THE SUMMER DARE

PART OF THE SUMMER IN SEASIDE SERIES

AMANDA SHELLEY

Visit my website at
www.amandashelley.com

CONNECT WITH AMANDA SHELLEY

Want to be the first to know about upcoming sales and new releases? Make sure you sign up for my newsletter as well as connect with me on social media and your favorite retail store.

Website:
www.amandashelley.com
Newsletter:
https://geni.us/AmandaShelleyNL
Facebook:
https://www.facebook.com/authoramandashelley/
Instagram:
https://www.instagram.com/authoramandashelley/
Reader's Group:
https://www.facebook.com/groups/AmandasArmyofReaders/
Tik Tok:
https://www.tiktok.com/@authoramandashelley
Amazon:
https://www.amazon.com/author/amandashelley
Goodreads:
https://www.goodreads.com/author/show/19713563.Amanda_Shelley

Book Bub:
https://www.bookbub.com/profile/amanda-shelley

ABOUT THE BOOK

Leave it to Nana to think of everything.

After a grueling semester, I'm ready for a peaceful summer in Seaside with my sisters.

Imagine my surprise, when I'm woken by the screeching sound of a saw coming through my wall, the first official morning of break.

Not only did I come flying out of bed swinging, but I gave Ryan, the unsuspecting carpenter the surprise of his life, when I came wielding my killer coat hanger and all.

Too bad, I was only in a tank and undies and it wasn't nearly as effective as I'd hoped.

Of course, he insists he's only doing his job. Since it's Nana's last request to care for us, I can't refuse.

However, I won't let a tall, pesky, sexy as sin, know-it-all get in my way of my summer plans. I pretend I ignore him - that is until my youngest sister pokes her nose in my business and throws down a dare I can't back down from.

Kiss the next single guy who walks up to the bonfire - or explain to my sisters why I get riled up over the contractor.

When Ryan suddenly appears, I know I'm screwed in more ways than one.

Not only will my sisters learn my secret, but from the determined look on Ryan's face, I'm afraid he's eager to reveal it to the world as well.

What have I gotten myself into?

As I walk toward him, one thing is certain - *this summer dare will either make or break me.*

Chapter 1
Lanie

IT'S LATE when I arrive at Nana's. I'm exhausted in more ways than I can count. It's been a hell of a semester, I've been driving for hours, and most of all, it hurts like hell that she's not here to greet me.

Summers in Seaside with Nana have always been special. It's the one place I've truly called home. It's where I learned to surf as a kid, drive as a teen, and experienced my first kiss. I've never lived here year-round, but I've spent enough time that I'd almost call myself a local.

As I pull into the rocky driveway, there's an ache in my chest that hasn't gone away since we lost her in January. As much as I love Seaside and want to be close to my memories of her, I'm not sure I'm ready to face them either.

I miss her terribly.

I've always loved Seaside, Oregon. It's been my home away from home, my sanctuary. I'm sure it's had everything to do with

Nana being our rock through the years. Our parents divorced when my sisters and I were barely enrolled in school. When Dad was deployed, Mom sent us out to the coast to spend time with Nana for a much-needed break. I'd feel the same way if I had four girls in the span of four years. Though how she managed to have Lizzy after the twins is beyond me. I love my sisters, but I can't imagine being in my mom's shoes and starting a family at my age.

Now that I'm older, I've put the pieces together. My poor mom got pregnant each and every time Dad came home on leave after they had me. It's no wonder their relationship didn't work out. First, they were so young when they got together. He met her on a weekend trip to visit his buddy at the college where Mom attended and I came along nine months later. They loved each other and thought they could make it work. But unfortunately, as time went on, they realized they wanted different things.

She basically sent Dad a *Dear John* letter, and it's something he's never quite gotten over. He hasn't had many serious relationships over the years—that we know of. So, we like to tease him about being married to the Air Force. He's been in for nearly twenty-two years and has no intentions of retiring until he hits thirty.

Even with my dad's deployments, they've somehow managed to co-parent us the best they can. With Dad stationed at Lewis–McChord these past few years, we've seen him often and have made up for lost time. Thankfully he's stateside for at least the next year. To my surprise, Lizzy moved in with him her senior year, when Mom picked up a job as a traveling nurse. She'll graduate in a few weeks and join us for another summer in Seaside.

Turning off the engine, I stare at the empty house. Nana always had various lights on timers so the place didn't appear vacant while she was gone, but it's late and they've turned off for the night. All that remains is the porch light she used to leave on when she knew we were coming.

God, I miss her so much. I'd give anything for her to open that screen door and fly down the steps in one of her infamous mumus we teased her about. She'd wrap her arms around me tightly and I didn't think I'd ever let go.

The twins won't be here for at least another week. I'd been eager to leave campus this afternoon and couldn't wait to officially start my summer vacation. Now, I'm second-guessing my need for spending time at Nana's alone. Before she passed, I often visited this quaint town, as it's only a few hours away from Columbia River University. It didn't matter if she was here or away on one of her many adventures...for as long as I could remember, she always had a room for each of us. She insisted this was our home, too, so we treated it as such. She even left it to the four of us in her will. Though I haven't stepped foot in the place since her funeral. I just haven't been ready.

Dad paid someone to winterize and take care of anything perishable left here after the service, but I'm certain he hasn't been here himself, either. Hell, I'm not sure it's been touched by anyone other than the monthly cleaning crew that keeps things from getting out of hand.

Letting out a heavy sigh, I swallow the lump forming in my throat.

Staring up at the porch, I can picture Nana with her hand on her hip waiting on me to join her. I can almost hear her laugh in the wind as she'd say, "Well, what are you waiting for, Lanie? That car won't empty itself."

God, I'm being ridiculous.

Staying in this car won't make things any easier.

With a fortifying breath, I push open the door. Determined to get this over with, I quickly gather my purse, phone, and anything else I can carry from the front seat. Before I can stall again, I rush up the three steps to the light blue door. After punching in the code on the keypad, the locks disengage and I walk into Nana's home.

Somehow, it still smells just as I remember, like vanilla and spice.

Someone must have one of her favorite air fresheners plugged in. She always stockpiled those when she found them on sale. I'm sure we'll have them for years to come. Nana always was such a sucker for a deal.

Before I get too lost in thought, I turn off the house alarm and flip on the hallway light.

Knowing it always bothered her when we dropped our things at the door, I take my things to my room upstairs. Flipping more lights on as I go, I make my way to my favorite room in the house. Most of the bedrooms have a view of the ocean from a window or a deck off the side of the house. However, this room, in particular, is my favorite because I not only get a great view but have a reading nook where I've spent countless hours getting lost in my favorite novels.

Dragging my fingers along the thick cushion, I stare out into the darkened sky. The back of Nana's house sits up against the well-lit pathway of the promenade, but I can't see much beyond that tonight. I've spent countless hours people-watching, daydreaming, and watching the waves in the distance from this very spot.

The shrill of my phone ringing makes me jump and my heart race out of my chest. I'd turned it up to be heard over the music I played in the car, but it's a bit of an overkill in this silent house.

Seeing Sloane's picture light up the screen, I'm all thumbs as I attempt to answer it and nearly drop it on the floor before finally swiping open the call.

My sister's concerned voice comes through the line. "Hey, Lanie, have you made it? Raven and I have been worried." Even though we talk daily, it's not the same as seeing them in person. I can't wait to see them. It's been way too long.

As I return to my car, I quickly assure her, "You can stop. I'm fine. In fact, I just pulled in."

"I still can't believe you wouldn't wait for one of us to go with you." She and Raven are finishing their sophomore year at Gonzaga and aren't finished with their semester until the end of next week. I know if they weren't focused on finals, they both would have dropped everything so I wouldn't be here alone this first time.

"I'll be okay. Besides—you know I had to be out of my

apartment by tomorrow, or I have to pay another month's rent. It just wasn't worth it."

"Lanie..." she draws out and I can almost picture her punching her fist into her hip. I know how she worries about us —it's just how she is. Though if she was traveling alone, I'd probably feel the same.

"Seriously, Sloane, I'm good."

I love my sisters. There's nothing any of them wouldn't do for me. But I need to process the loss of Nana in my own way. I miss her like crazy, but the only way I'll truly get through this is by taking this first step—and that means continuing the life Nana would want me to live.

Hearing a heavy sigh from Sloane, I can tell she wants to say more, but instead, she changes the subject. "Have you heard from Lizzy today?"

"No. Not today. What's up?"

"I don't know... I haven't heard from her either. I thought she might have checked in with you."

I love how close we are as sisters, but I'm sure as a senior in high school, it can be a bit stifling to essentially have four moms. "I'm sure she's fine. If we don't hear from her in a few days, then we can worry. But you remember that age—you hated checking in, too."

Once outside, I'm reminded just how full my car is. *Why the hell did I pack so much?*

"Look, Sloane, I'm beat after moving today. I gotta unload my car."

"Okay... I'll call you after work tomorrow evening. If you hear from Liz, text me."

"Will do. Love you."

I have plenty of time to contemplate why the hell I brought so much crap, as I spend nearly an hour unloading my car. I blame it on moving apartments next fall. As I packed, I'd been unwilling to put some of my prized possessions in storage —like my photo albums and evidently, all of my clothes.

Unfortunately, the weather in Seaside doesn't always cooperate and prove it's actually summer—so I brought many of my sweats, hoodies, jeans, and warmer clothes along with things I'd wear in the summer, too. Which means I've packed entirely too much.

When I finish unpacking, I pull my car into the garage, parking beside Nana's classic convertible. How she used to love riding with the top down the moment the sun came out. Closing my eyes, I fondly remember our many rides along the coast with her scarf blowing in the breeze. Even though it's a happy memory, I quickly leave the garage to keep from dwelling on the thought. After dumping the last of my things in my room, I head to the kitchen for reinforcements. Nana always kept our favorite wine in the fridge and I'm certain there is still an unopened bottle in there when we last visited.

Opening the fridge, I'm relieved to find Nana still hasn't let me down.

Within minutes, the bottle's open and I've poured myself a large glass. Walking into the living room, I sink into my favorite end of her couch. I should finish unpacking my bags, but I need a breather. As I listen to the constant whir of the wind and waves crashing against the shore outside, I understand why Nana would often sit and do the same. Not wanting to get lost in my past or contemplate a future without her, I clear my mind and simply exist in this moment. A sense of peace washes over me as I sip my Moscato. It's like I can feel her presence and she's still here watching over me.

I'm not sure how long I stay in this state, but before I know it, my glass is empty. Reluctantly, I pull myself back to reality and head to the kitchen. After refilling my glass of wine, I return to my room, grab a hanger, and get to work.

By the time I slip into my sheets, my eyes will barely stay open. I'm not sure which had a greater effect—the wine or the stress of the day. Either way, I'm beat. I'm not even sure my head hits the pillow before I fall into a coma-like sleep.

I don't even dream. I'm that tired.

That is until a scene from a horror movie I watched as a kid comes to life.

Bolting straight out of bed to the sound of a chainsaw coming through the house, I'm on my feet in an instant.

What. The. Actual. Fuck?

Someone's breaking into the house—with a chainsaw?

This cannot be happening.

My heart pounds through my chest as I grab the nearest weapon I can get my hands on and rush to the stairs. There's no way I'm going down without a fight.

As soon as my feet hit the floor in the living room, I realize the sound is actually outside on the front deck, but I'm still not having it. There's no way in hell I'm letting anyone do anything to Nana's house if I can help it. This place is everything to me.

Swinging open the door so hard that it nearly rips off the hinge, I stomp onto the front deck. As soon as I spot the culprit leaning against the wall using a tool that is most definitely *NOT* a chainsaw to cut at the house—I scream above the noise. "What the hell do you think you're doing?"

The cutting continues as if he hasn't heard a word I said.

Spotting the extension cord on the opposite side of the deck, I march over on a mission and unplug it. Instantly the shrilling machine silences and a low oath rips from the man's lips as he inspects his machine before locating the cord.

His eyes widen and he stands to his full height. Holy shit. I didn't think this through. He's considerably taller than me, but I'm too angry to care.

Swinging the coat hanger in his direction for emphasis, I shout, "Just what the hell do you think you're doing?"

He eyes me up and down and then lands on the coat hanger I'm wielding in my hand as his hands drop to his sides and a smirk forms on his face. His shoulders straighten and his chin juts out as one brow raises in speculation. "Shouldn't I be asking you that question?"

"This is my house and you're trespassing," I remind him with authority.

"No, I'm not." He crosses his arms over his broad chest, yet doesn't let go of the tool he's carrying.

"Yes, you are. You're not only trespassing, but you're also disturbing the fucking peace."

Damn. Just how tall is this guy? He can't be much older than me, and I'm fairly certain he's not dangerous, but even from the distance I've kept between us, I'm forced to crane my neck up to look him in the eye.

Before I can let his height detour me, I continue my rant. "You have no right being on my property, let alone destroying it at the fucking ass-crack of dawn," I spit out like a petulant child. "Here I am, enjoying my first full day of summer, only to be woken to the sound of a saw coming through my fucking wall. Just who the hell do you think you are?"

His jaw ticks for a few moments, then a heavy breath is released.

"First, it's not the ass-crack of dawn. It's already seven-thirty and the sun's been out for hours. Second, I've been hired by Jane Lancaster to do some renovations on the place, so I'm clearly not destroying it."

At the mention of my grandmother's name, I hesitate for the briefest of moments and mutter, "That's... not possible."

"I assure you, it is," he firmly states, looking down at me from his towering height. His muscles twitch under his well-fitted black t-shirt. He's not bulky, but he isn't a string bean, as Nana would say, either. No, he fills out his lengthy form perfectly.

Taking a breath, I stammer out the words I hate to admit. "That's... really... not possible. She's been gone... since... January." My chest aches as if those words are once again a finality that Nana's really gone.

Clenching his jaw, he sighs heavily. I watch impatiently as his eyes dart to the hanger in my hand, then down my body before returning to meet my gaze. "Look, I've got the contract in my truck," he starts out forcefully, then looks to the sky before adding, "Can you put on some pants, so we can talk about this? And maybe stow your killer coat hanger while you're at it. I don't mean you any harm."

Chapter 2
Ryan

WHEN I MENTION her lack of pants, all the wind momentarily drops from her sails. Her fierceness droops and her cheeks darken, but somehow she remains standing tall. She's got a rockin' body—but unfortunately her freak flag is flying—so it's best if my mind doesn't go there.

I mean—who uses a coat hanger for protection? There has to be a million things she could've grabbed on her way out. I must've scared the piss out of her, for her to come out screaming like a banshee brandishing *that* as a weapon.

I can't blame her. No one wants to be woken like this.

But I've got a job to do.

I need to finish this project, so I can move on to the next and get this dreadful summer over with. Working at my family's company is the last thing I want—I certainly don't have time to deal with a pretentious princess.

After watching her nod once and say, "I'll be right back,"

she turns on a dime and stomps into the house. She's wearing tiny boy shorts as underwear and her toned legs look amazing on her retreat. Not to mention, her beautifully round ass... Holy hell, it's the perfect combination of sway and jiggle as she firmly retreats.

Fuck, man. Get it together.

Shaking my head, I walk to my truck so I can find the necessary paperwork to show her I am in fact NOT an intruder and the entire scene plays on repeat in my mind. If I wasn't so irritated that her tantrum was putting me behind schedule, I'd probably find it funny.

I've seen a lot of things on the job, but this by far takes the cake. I kinda like her inability to back down. Her darkened cheeks were her only sign of being embarrassed. I'm fairly certain if she'd been fully dressed, I would've had my ass handed to me this morning because clearly, she was just getting started.

She's not short but compared to me, I dwarf her. I'm six-six and she barely stands at my shoulders. Her hair was stacked on her head in a messy bun, and it flopped as she shook her head at me. Her face was free from makeup, and her expressive blue eyes made it hard to look away.

As soon as I find the contract I'm looking for, I slam my truck door shut and return to the scene of the crime. I'm sure this is just a misunderstanding that we can sort out—like rational adults.

Surely, she won't stay mad forever, right?

At twenty-two, I'm used to not being taken seriously. But I've been on job sites like this since I was fourteen. My dad taught me the ropes from the time I could walk. Now that I've just finished my junior year of college and have only one year left in completing my construction-management degree, I'd say I'm more than capable of a simple project like this.

With the weather expected to hold out for the week, I'm pulling off the siding from the most weathered side of the house, then I'll have a few members of my father's crew help me replace it. Typically, we're not alone on a job, but Jared had a family emergency and I can do this part of the job by myself—as long as that feisty girl inside cooperates.

When she returns a few minutes later, I'm relieved to find she's wearing a pair of leggings and a baggy sweatshirt. It's sad to see her beautiful body covered, but it's far less distracting.

I hand her my copy of the contract. "As you can see, Jane Lancaster paid us last fall—in full—to redo her siding, roof, and replace both the floor and tub in the master bathroom. So..." I draw out to prove my point. "I am—in fact—entitled to be here."

Shaking her head, she mutters, "This is so like Nana. She always thought of everything."

"Nana?" I ask, not wanting to make assumptions. If she's not here to oversee this herself, where is she? I know for a fact the front office confirmed this project—it's protocol. I wouldn't be here otherwise or have the code for the alarm.

"She's my grandma..." The woman bites on her lip then sighs heavily. "Well, was my grandma. We lost her in January."

Grief radiates from her features and not only does my chest tighten, but eventually my manners kick in. "Sorry for your loss..." Shit, I don't even know her name.

Needing to rectify this, I clear my throat and stick out my hand. "I think we've gotten off to a bad start. I'm Ryan Murdock." When she doesn't take my hand, I press the issue further, "And you are?"

"I'm... Melanie Lancaster." Her lower lip slips under her teeth and she looks to the siding I've begun removing before glancing to the roof then she mutters, "Would it have killed her to keep us in the loop?"

Yeah, I'm thinking that's a rhetorical question—or at least one I'm not touching with a ten-foot pole. I don't know why her grandma planned this reno so far in advance. I know we were booked pretty far out this past year, and sure these things need replacing, but they still have a couple of years left on them. Then again, we are at the coast and it's best not to let things get dilapidated if you want to keep damage minimal.

Thankfully, Lanie answers her own question with a shake of her head. "It's just like her... doing these things so my sisters and I wouldn't have to deal with it later. Nana always thought of everything."

"She sounds like a smart woman," I add, not knowing what else to say.

Lanie's slow smile makes me wonder what else she's thinking.

On a nod, she agrees. "Yeah. She was." Her grandma must've been one hell of a lady.

"So..." I draw out, wondering where she's at with the project. "Are you good with me continuing the job?"

Cocking her head to the side, she places her hand on her

hip and stares up at me. "Are you gonna keep waking me up at the ass-crack of dawn with that hideous tool each day?"

"I've only got so many hours of daylight," I pointedly remind her.

"In my defense, you scared the crap out of me. Here I was in a dreamless and peaceful sleep on my first official day of summer... and suddenly I thought you were coming through the walls." She cringes and my heart sinks when I realize I've totally traumatized her. "I seriously thought you were the Texas Chainsaw Massacre or something."

"Please tell me you didn't watch those movies as a kid." I cringe remembering my cousin forcing me to watch scary movies with him.

Shaking her head, she laughs. "No... not as a kid. A freshman in college... and that was scary enough. My roommate went away and I didn't sleep the entire weekend."

Yeah, I'm not ready to relive that particular movie either, though she doesn't need to know that bit of information.

"But back to the subject. This is my first day of summer and there's no way in hell I want another morning like this."

"Okay, how about this..." I start with a compromise. "I'll promise not to start any machinery until eight if you don't mind I'm here earlier to prep things. I'll stay out of your hair the best I can, but I can't make any promises that I won't inconvenience you. There are only so many sunny days in Seaside without rain. I need to take advantage of them while I can." Then I glance at the overhang above me and realize not everything is under my control, so I quickly amend, "However, when we get to the roof, it will entirely depend on when the rest of the crew is available. Though we should knock that out in a couple of days if we get everyone on it."

"Now that I know you're coming, I won't be as traumatized," she admits.

A phone rings from inside the house, but before she rushes off to get it, I grab her attention once more, "And, Melanie... you can leave your killer coat hanger in the closet. I promise I don't mean you any harm."

For a moment she just closes her eyes and lets out a heavy breath.

When her phone rings again, she quickly shakes her head and rushes away without a word.

Chapter 3
Lanie

WHAT AN ASS.

Not willing to dignify him a response, I rush to my phone shaking my head at his pointed reminder of just how stupid he must think I am.

Next time, I'll grab a bat. I'm sure we have one of those around here somewhere.

Though I'm grateful to Nana for taking care of things—even from the grave. I'm not sure how I feel about strangers being around all summer.

So much for a peaceful, stress-free summer.

When I finally get to my phone, I'm breathless, but I manage to catch it before voice mail picks it up. "Hey, Dad, what's up?"

"Hey, Lanie. I meant to call you earlier this week, but I've been out in the field for training... and you know how that goes. Apparently, Mom's still up to her old tricks. I had a contractor reach out to inform me she's arranged for some things to be done at the beach house this summer. She was presumptuous enough to think we couldn't handle things without her, so she took it upon herself to pay for all the renovations upfront, including scheduling them. They should be starting in the next day or so."

Yeah, a heads up would have been nice.

"Yeah... they... started this morning."

I'm not about to tell Dad how I rushed outside in my underwear, with only a hanger. I'd never hear the end of it. Sure, I've taken martial arts since I was old enough to walk. He's always made sure my sisters and I can handle ourselves, but I'm not about to have him show up unexpectedly or insist I come stay with him until my sisters can be here with me. He's always been protective, even from afar.

No, thank you. I'm an adult and I can handle simple things like renovations. It's not like I haven't lived alone for the past few years. Besides, I've already got a summer job lined up, and I won't miss out on potential tips.

That's just not happening.

"Really? Shit... that's what I get for putting things off." I can picture him shaking his head in frustration at himself. Dad doesn't usually drop the ball; he's a lot like Nana in that—so he must've had a reason not to call. "I didn't want to bother you as you were finishing up your summer class... and with all the activities your sister has going on with graduation... I should've made the time. There's no excuse."

"Dad, it's fine. Really. I'm here and I can handle things." Even if said things are ginormously tall, sexy, and brooding.

I'm sure Ryan's bark is much worse than his bite, but I'll handle anything he throws my way.

Dad says something about knowing that I can handle things, but my mind is on Ryan.

Is he always a grumpy giant? Or is there more to him?

Focus, Lanie.

Now is not the time to think about this. Especially with your dad on the other end of the line.

Quickly, I pull myself together and relay what Ryan said to appease my father. "Since the weather is supposed to hold off this week they're starting with the siding. I'm not sure when the roof will be done, but it will all work out."

"Do you think we should postpone Lizzy's party in a couple of weeks?"

"No. I'm sure things will work out. Besides, you've only got so much leave and we've already invited everyone. Even if the house is under construction, I'm sure they don't work Sundays, right?" I've already cleared that weekend off with my boss and I'm not about to change our plans now—even if Nana has other intentions.

"I'm not sure..." Dad draws out and I can easily picture him chewing on his lower lip like I do when I'm deep in thought.

"Look, I'll talk with Ryan and get things sorted."

"Ryan?" Dad asks with interest.

"He's the contractor I spoke with just now."

"Okay. I'll leave things up to you. But if you need anything, you know where to find me."

Like I don't have his number on speed-dial.

"I know, Dad." I draw out for his benefit.

"Look, I got a meeting in five minutes. You sure you're good?"

"Go. Do your thing. I'm fine," I insist. "Besides, I start work in the morning. I can't spend the day relaxing at the beach unless I get started ASAP," I tease, using Nana's favorite saying when we visited.

This brings a laugh from Dad. "Sure thing, kiddo. I'll talk to you soon. Don't forget sunscreen."

"Yes, Dad," I draw out. Which earns me another laugh as I make my way back upstairs to get ready for a day at the beach. It's not overly warm here in the Pacific Northwest, but there's no rain, so I'll take it.

After hanging up with Dad, I quickly change into a pair of jean cut-off shorts and a loose-fitting tee and grab a hoodie.

I take a few minutes in the bathroom to run a brush through my hair, only to put it back into a messy bun. I'm not sure why I bother but it makes me feel better to know I've at least tried once for the day. By the time I brush my teeth and head back downstairs, I'm starving.

I should've gone shopping. But I'll settle with dropping into a restaurant in town before I head off hungry to the market. Who the hell knows what I'll end up with if I hangry shop.

As I grab my purse and walk out the back deck, I spot Ryan coming from his truck. "Hey. Do you want me to leave the door open, so you can use the restroom or anything?"

Raising a brow, he grimaces. "Do you make a habit of leaving your place unlocked?"

"Not usually." It comes out snarkier than I intend. "But I'll only be gone for a bit and I thought I'd be polite. If you're renovating the bathrooms, you already have access to the place, right?"

Sighing heavily, he crosses his arms. "Yes. As a matter of fact, I do. But that doesn't mean you should be leaving your door unlocked."

Okay, Mr. Grumpy Pants, point taken.

Raising a brow of my own in challenge, I say, "With you working out here, I doubt anyone will bother the place. But if you'd rather have to find the key so you can pee, be my guest. It was my *attempt* at being hospitable. *Obviously,* I've made a mistake." Exaggeratedly, I click the lock on the door and slam it shut.

"Christ, that's not what I meant," he mutters.

Turning on a dime to face him, I ask, "What *did* you mean then?"

Shaking his head, he mutters, "Nothing. It's none of my business."

"Then why did you say anything?" I hedge as I stare at him waiting for a response.

Taking a deep breath, he finally meets my eyes. "Look, you're here—alone and I don't want you taking any unnecessary risks, for my sake."

"Seaside is a pretty safe place," I remind him.

"Not the point," he grumbles then shakes his head. "Sorry. I appreciate the gesture. But I'd rather use my key to the back door if you'll be gone long. I'd rather you keep it locked in case

I suddenly get pulled to our other job site in town or have to run and get something."

That makes sense.

"I'm just running down the boardwalk to grab something for breakfast. Then I'll likely grab some things at the store on my way home. Need anything while I'm out?"

Why the hell am I asking him that?

It's not like I owe him anything.

"Uh... no. I'm good, thanks." Reaching for his phone, he swipes it open. "Would you mind if I got your number so I can keep you up to date on everything? I'll shoot you a quick text, so you can have mine, too, if you need anything."

Since he'll be here for the foreseeable future, it makes sense. Quickly, I rattle off my number, then I hear a notification ping from my phone shortly after he hits the final button.

Grinning, he says, "Thanks. Enjoy your breakfast, Melanie." And with that, he moves past me up the deck to get back to work.

"It's Lanie," I state as a peace offering. "I'm only called Melanie when I'm in trouble or when solicitors call."

Without waiting for a response, I bounce down the steps and walk toward breakfast.

I swear I feel his eyes follow me as I retreat, but I refuse to glance his way to check like my body wants to.

Chapter 4
Ryan

WOULD *you mind if I got your number so I can keep you up to date on everything? I'll shoot you a quick text, so you can have mine, too, if you need anything.*

Gah, could I be *more* lame?

Seriously. It's like I'd been transformed into an awkward pre-teen asking my crush for their number. With her being the only local contact for this job, it made sense to get it, but I could've been a little smoother in asking her.

And why the hell do I care if she leaves her door unlocked? It's not like hundreds of locals around town don't do it daily.

Hell, I have no idea.

But for some reason, I felt protective.

Which makes zero sense.

Other than scaring the crap out of her this morning and her grandmother dying, I know nothing about her.

So why am I still obsessing over her?

Somehow, I've managed to clear nearly all of the siding from the lower part of the wall I'd been working on by the time I spot her walking up the path from town.

Holy crap. How much did she buy at the store? Her arms are loaded and I swear they're teetering on the brink of spilling across the pavement.

Hopping off the deck, I rush to close the distance between us. "Here, let me help you," I offer, reaching for a bag to lighten her load.

"Thanks," she mutters, handing over another, then readjusting the load she's carrying to balance the weight of her purchases.

"Have you ever thought of driving to the store?" I ask, taking another bag from her when I see she's struggling to open the door.

Blowing out a breath of air, she huffs, "Yes." Then she quickly continues, "I only went to pick up a few things—and obviously, things got a little out of hand."

"You could've called," flies out of my mouth before I can stop myself.

What the hell am I doing?

She stops in her tracks and stares at me as if I've said the most ridiculous thing she's ever heard.

"Or not..." I mutter. "You go right ahead and heft your groceries over a mile home. Who am I to stop you?"

Eying me suspiciously, she sets a bag on the kitchen counter. "Would you really have done that?"

"Why not?" I shrug. It's not like I'm a complete ass or anything. Besides who the hell loads themselves down with groceries without bringing their car?

I haven't seen a car in the driveway, so maybe she doesn't have one.

"Uh, you don't know me from Adam and you're under no obligation to do anything but renovate our house."

She's right. I don't. Yet, I admit another truth. "It doesn't mean I want you to struggle."

"Well... thanks... I guess." Then she shakes her head and mutters, "Next time I'll remember my car. I doubt I'll have feeling in my fingers for the rest of the day." She busies herself by putting away the groceries, and I'm left rocking on my heels.

"Well, I'll just leave you to it. That siding won't remove itself."

Looking up from her bag, she gives me a beautiful smile. "Thanks, Ryan."

For a moment we just stare at one another.

My mouth dries and I get lost in the moment far longer than I should. But before I can say anything else entirely inappropriate, I simply nod once and high tail it out of there.

Needing to get as far away from her as possible, I beeline it to my truck and grab the water bottle I'd packed this morning. Taking a large swig from my hydro flask, I'm relieved to find the water still as icy as when I'd filled it this morning. It does nothing to quench my sudden thirst. But the coolness manages to clear my head.

Staring at the house before me I nearly spill the contents of the bottle when the sudden shrill of my phone fills the cab. Hastily, I grab for my phone without looking at the caller ID. "Murdock."

"Bad time?" My father's voice booms through the phone.

"Nope. Just grabbing a drink of water," I admit, taking a steadying breath.

"Jared's not gonna be available until tomorrow. You alright for the rest of the day?"

"Yeah. I've got a few things I can work on before calling it a day. Will he make it in tomorrow?"

"Not sure. His younger brother was in some sort of trouble and Jared had to take him outside of Portland to get things sorted. I didn't get the details, but he mentioned he'd be back in a day or two."

"Welp," I say, running a hand over my jaw. "I've got plenty to do. As you always say, family comes first, so I don't begrudge him for steppin' in."

"Need me to drive out there to give you a hand?"

Dad's doing a job about an hour away and there's nothing he can help me with today, so I let him off the hook. "Nah. I'm good. I'll reach out to Jared when I get home this evening to make a plan for the rest of this week."

"Alright." Dad's deep voice quips. "You know where to find me. I'll check in with you later."

Before I can even respond, the line goes dead. Knowing Dad, he's likely already onto his next call by now. We've undertaken a lot of jobs this summer and we're stretched pretty thin for a small company. But it's nothing we haven't handled before.

As much as I wish my job had worked out in Boston this summer, I'm glad I'm able to help fill the void of my uncle Frank retiring earlier this year. I know for a fact my dad needs me, even if it means I don't get to travel as much as I'd hoped.

Just as I hop onto the deck to take off more siding, the door to the house swings open and Lanie comes out carrying a bag for the beach and a lawn chair over her shoulder. "Oh, hey there, I didn't see you."

"I took a call in my truck."

"Well, I've got a date with the sand, the waves, and my book." Turning to lock the door, she smiles. "I've locked up, but the alarm's not set, if you need anything inside."

Then she rolls her eyes and smirks—as if she thinks she's just gotten the last word.

What a smartass. Two can play this game.

Not wanting to show she's affecting me, I nod once and reply, "I'm taking off around four. If I don't see you, enjoy your first official day of summer."

As I walk by, she pats me on the arm. "Well, it was nice meeting you, Ryan. Even if you did scare the piss out of me. Now that I know you're here, I promise to keep my weapons stowed."

So that's how she wants to play it.

"Good to know. I'll be ready, should you come charging at me again."

The vixen winks. "Somebody's gotta keep you on your toes."

Then she bounces down the stairs and along the path that heads to the shore. Once again, I'm left staring at her for much longer than I care to admit, as she crests over the grassy sand dune and disappears behind it.

I'm not sure what's gotten into me, but for the first time since returning from Boston, I'm looking forward to coming to work tomorrow.

Chapter 5
Ryan

SINCE IT'S JUST me again on the job, and I promised Lanie I wouldn't run any power tools until eight, I don't bother showing up until seven-thirty. One of the perks of managing my own crew is setting my own hours. Though I'd rather get the job started and be done with my day, I stop for some coffee at one of the drive-thru stands on my way to work.

Unloading the scaffolding near the deck, I decide I'll tackle the top of the weathered wall I'd started yesterday. I managed to clear everything under the eave, but I can't wait any longer to do the top.

Just as I set the last bit of frame alongside the house, a blood-curdling scream comes from within.

Holy shit. That's Lanie.

Racing around the side of the house, I jump up the steps and I'm at the door in no time, where the screams only get louder.

"Stop... Oh, shit... NO... NO... NO!!!"

What the fuck?

Without knocking, I reach for my key and have the door opened in seconds.

"Lanie?" I holler, breaching the house.

"In here..." comes a desperate cry.

It takes all of two steps inside to witness the fiasco ensuing.

What the fuck?

Lanie's ineffectively holding a towel in front of her to keep the water from spraying herself as well as the entire kitchen. Oh, shit, the faucet's broken at the handle and the water's hitting her at full force.

Springing into action, I'm careful not to slip as I scurry to turn off the water at the cutoff valve. The sink is fairly new, but the plumbing underneath isn't. Christ, this sucker won't budge.

"Hang on!" I holler as I dart outside to grab a wrench from my toolbox and try again.

"This fucker doesn't wanna move," I grunt in frustration as water continues to assault the room from above.

Trying a new angle, I use the full force of my weight until finally—it turns.

The streaming water from above slows. The moment it shuts off, I hear Lanie let out a deep breath.

As I emerge from under the sink, it's then I notice her long muscular legs standing beside me. She's at least got pants on— if you consider sleep shorts pants. But compared to yesterday, it's better than nothing.

However, her light pink tank is drenched and does nothing to conceal her erect nipples.

I do my best to avert my eyes.

But I'm a guy.

I notice her beautiful pert breasts standing at attention. If dry, the fabric would do its job, but wet—yeah—that leaves little to the imagination.

And she has perfect breasts.

Round, plump, and more than a handful.

I am so fucking screwed.

"Ohmigod, thank you," she gushes as she rushes to a cabinet to get some towels. "I'm so glad you're here."

"No problem," I offer instinctually. Noting there aren't nearly enough towels, I offer, "Where are the bathroom towels?"

"In the hall, second door on the right," she says, pointing off to the kitchen.

Darting in that direction, I hear her add, "I'm so glad you got here, I tried to turn off the valve but it wouldn't budge. I was just about to give up and go look for a tool chest when you barged in. I can't thank you enough for showing up when you did."

"Let's get this cleaned up then inspect the damage. If you want, I'll fix it first thing this morning," I offer, dropping to my knees to soak up the small lake that's formed in the kitchen.

Shit. There's a lot of water here. How long had this been gushing?

When she's quiet and doesn't move I glance her way.

She hesitantly looks from the sink to me, then back to the sink before asking, "You sure?"

Nodding, I get back to work before too much damage is done. "What do you think general contractors are for?"

"Are you sure it won't be too much trouble?"

"Nope. Do you happen to have a wet/dry vac? It might be easier than sopping this mess up with towels."

Looking toward the garage, she hesitates. "I have no idea. But I'll check."

With a limited amount of towels, I make quick work of scooping up a sopping wet one, quickly wring out the excess water, then throw it on the floor to keep the water contained. It may be a vain attempt, but as I scurry between towels, I hope like hell it soaks up more water in the process.

When the door to the garage bangs open with a giant shop vac in her hands, Lanie huffs, "I've got this. Will it work?"

Relieved, I rush to her. "Absolutely. Let's make sure it's empty and the filter's off before we put this sucker to work." Feeling its weight, I ask, "Do you have a garbage bag?"

Rushing to the sink, she grabs a large trash bag. I empty the contents and filter and within minutes, and water's finally coming off the floor. With the roar of the machine, between us, we wordlessly work together. She keeps the mess from spreading by taking my lead from before and wringing out the towels and creating barriers to contain the excess water around us.

The moment I click off the machine, my ears ring in the silence, though I manage to hear Lanie exhale as if she's exhausted. "Ah... thank God, this is almost over."

As I reach for a towel, my arm brushes against hers and I quickly mutter, "Sorry," when I see her shiver in response.

Standing with a puzzled expression she asks, "What the hell do you have to be sorry for? You literally just saved my house from being flooded." She slowly looks me over from head to toe before adding, "If anything, I'm the one that should be apologizing. You and I are both soaked to the bone. Please tell me you at least have a change of clothes nearby."

"Uh, I can't say it's real close, but my place is just outside of town—so is anything really that far in Seaside? I'll swing by and change before heading to get a faucet."

I really hope I brought another pair of boots with me for the summer because these will be miserable to wear the rest of the day. Maybe if I set them out in the sun, they'll dry before I return to the job site.

Lanie glances at the clock on the stove and groans as she gathers the towels from the sink. "Shoot. I've gotta get ready for work. Do you think it will be okay to take a shower and wash this load of towels or is the water gonna be turned off?"

Chuckling at the disgruntled expression on her face, I assure her. "You'll be fine. The water is only turned off at the sink. If I need to shut off the main, I'll do it when you're done."

Shaking her head, she grumbles, "I may as well wash what I can of these, so I can shower and get to work on time. I hope to God there are towels upstairs, or I'm screwed." Loading her arms with wet towels, she awkwardly carries them so they're a safe distance from her body.

Yeah, it's best I don't respond to that comment. There's no way I want her day to be worse than it's started. Seeing she can't take all the towels in one trip, I load up my own arms with the rest and follow her to the laundry room.

She quickly shoves her load in the wash and turns to mine. "I'd better wash more than one load. Just throw those in the utility sink and I'll do it later."

Slipping past her, I do as she says.

As I turn to exit the laundry room, she turns at the same time in my direction. She startles at our closeness but then freezes and her eyes remain pinned to the center of my soaked chest. When she doesn't move or say anything I break the now uncomfortable silence with, "Lanie? You okay?"

Shaking her head, she quickly inhales. "Yeah. Just... lost for a moment."

"Okay..." I draw out, wondering what's going on in that head of hers.

When her eyes slowly rise to meet mine she says, "Thanks again..." Her voice is raspy so she clears it. "For your help, that is. Are you sure you have time to fix that sink today? I really can call someone else."

"There's no need to hire anyone when I can easily do the repair job."

Rolling her lip between her teeth she looks to our feet before returning to meet my gaze. "But I'm not sure what Nana's prepaid you. Will you let me know the cost so I can figure out a way to pay you?"

Christ, is that what she's worried about?

"Look. I'll add it to the bill and if it puts us over our budget, I'll let you know as we finish the project and we can work things out then. It won't be too much to add a faucet to the project we're already involved with."

"Okay. But you'll tell me *before* you come even close to going over budget, right?"

"Of course." Though it won't be a problem.

Maybe my immediate agreement to her demand throws her off because she suddenly clamps her mouth into a straight line and nods once.

When she still doesn't move, I ask, "Are we good then?"

Crossing her arms over her chest she nods once and turns on a dime and returns to the kitchen only to look at the clock and groan. "Shit. I can't be late today."

Apologetically, she somehow smiles. "I really gotta run. Text me if you need anything, okay?"

"Same with you," I pointedly remind her. "I'm just glad I got here when I did, or there'd be even more damage."

"Ugg... don't remind me."

"I'll head out now and see what we can get in terms of faucets. I might need to run into Warden or Astoria to get something similar. Will you be here when I return?"

Shaking her head, she shrugs. "Nah. I'll be working until way after you get off."

Nodding once in agreement, I walk toward the door. Pulling it open, I pause and holler to get her attention, "Hey, Lanie?"

"Yeah?" She pauses with one foot on the staircase.

"Good luck with your first day of work. I'm sure all the crazy shit is behind you."

Without waiting for a response, I turn and walk out the door.

Chapter 6
Ryan

IT'S BEEN a shit day and I need a good meal and a drink. I had to go to three different stores before I could find a faucet similar to the one in the kitchen. And of course—nothing at the coast is close and everyone and their grandpa has to chat my ear off and check in to see how my dad's doing.

It's times like this I wish my internship in Boston had worked out this summer. There was something to be said about being unknown. Though I found out there's a flip-side to that coin as well. Being unknown also meant everyone questioned my authority, especially the owner's son who was constantly inserting himself where it didn't belong. He had shit for brains and impeded the project with his unsafe practices. When I brought this up with the boss, I quickly realized I wasn't able to do the job I was hired for. There was no way I'd be learning anything in that environment, so I quit and came back home for the summer to take more responsibility with my dad's company.

I'd rather diversify my experience, especially if I want to expand my horizons by going into larger commercial projects, but my dad trusts my work and this is a reputable company in this business. He'd have my ass if I pulled the shit Don's son did.

Pulling into Pop's Hops, my favorite bar, my stomach growls. I spent the better part of the day fixing Lanie's sink. To make up for some lost time, I've worked a few hours later than usual, and it's now after six. I'm looking forward to one of Pop's famous steak dinners and an ice-cold microbrew to unwind from the day.

It takes a few minutes for my eyes to adjust from the brightness of the day as I enter, but I hear a woman's voice holler over the soft music in the background. "Welcome to Pop's. You're welcome to seat yourself and I'll be right with you."

I swear that voice sounds familiar, but then again, Seaside's only so big. Like my errands today, when you grow up around here, you're bound to run into people you know. Slipping into the restroom down a back hall, I take a minute to wash my hands and clean up. There's no way in hell, I want the grime of the day sticking with my meal.

After the sink fiasco this morning, I'd changed into another pair of jeans and one of my older CRU t-shirts—but I'd hate to ruin it completely. I'd gotten it long before I was even accepted to Columbia River—in hopes of getting into my dream university. The moment I heard about their construction-management program, I had been hooked.

Walking back into the bar, I slide into a small booth for two. This way I won't take a bigger table for tourists. I also know it's out of the way—I've had more than my share of small talk for the day, and I don't need to be recognized by any more old-time locals. Like me, most of my friends are long gone from Seaside. We didn't waste any time getting out to spread our wings, as my dad would say. Unless you love tourism or run a family business, there's not a lot of employment opportunities that hold long-term potential—so most of us left and only return to visit family.

Once seated, I take a moment to lean back and stretch my legs out. *Fuck, it's been one hell of a day.* Closing my eyes, I rest my head against the wall behind me to recharge. Hopefully, Jared returns tomorrow and we can kick ass to get caught up. If not, I may need to pull someone from Dad's crew because I'm running out of things I can do on my own with the siding. Sooner or later, I need help on that second level.

"Thanks for waiting," startles me out of my musing over the job site. "I'm Lanie. Can I get you anything to drink while you look over the menu?"

Of all the places I could've walked into.

Just hearing her familiar voice brings a smile to my lips. Suddenly my exhaustion from the day disappears and I sit forward to greet her.

"Well, fancy meeting you here," I muse.

God, she looks even more beautiful than I remember. Her makeup is minimal, but that doesn't mean I don't take notice.

Her expressive eyes are lined making them pop and her lashes look longer. Her hair is pulled into one of her adorable messy buns and she's wearing a black tank that has Pop's Hops written in bright yellow script across her chest. I've seen the logo countless times, but I'm certain no one wears it better than her.

The tank is tucked into a pair of black Capri jeans and the silver from her belt buckle peeks out at the center of her waist. Her lips curve into a lopsided grin when she says, "Shouldn't I be saying that? I'm the one who works here." Lifting a pad from her apron, she asks, "Need a menu, or do you already know what you want?"

Glancing at the specialties on the sign above the left side of the bar, I quickly say, "I'll take a pint of the Puckering Pear and a steak, medium, with a baked potato and steamed broccoli."

"Want the works on the potato?"

Nodding, she writes something on the pad. "I hear the Puckering Pear is new this year from Bed Knobs and Brews in Colorado. Is it any good?"

Raising a brow, I tease, "You work here and haven't tasted it?"

"Well, it is my first day," she points out. "It's not like I can drink on the job or anything."

"Point taken." I shrug. "You'll have to try it one day. It's incredible."

"For now, I'll take your word for it." She glances at her watch then asks, "Wait, are you just now getting off work?"

Sighing heavily, I stick with the truth. "Yeah. Your sink is completely fixed and I tackled what I could of the siding before leaving. If Jared isn't back tomorrow, I'll pull someone from another crew to get started with the top of your house. We've only got so many days of sun this coming week and I don't wanna be up there when the weather changes."

"I feel bad that you were put behind because of me."

"Don't worry about it. I'm still making progress."

Something catches her attention on my chest, and she gasps. *Crap, did I miss something on my quick inspection just now?*

"Wait? Were you a fan of CRU before or after they won their second D-1 basketball championship last year?"

Smirking at her need to clarify, only a true fan of CRU would even ask that. "I'd say before, as I only have one year left to complete my degree."

Her jaw drops and forms the perfect O.

When she simply stares, self-consciousness trickles in the longer she remains silent. "Did I say something wrong?"

"Where did you live freshman year?"

"Coleman Hall?" comes out as a question because I'm so confused by her line of thoughts.

"Which floor?"

"Eighth."

These are oddly specific questions.

Shaking her head with disbelief clearly written across her features she mutters, and I barely make out, "No way."

"You gonna fill me in, or do you get a kick out of keeping me in the dark?"

Slowly she nods her head and exhales heavily. "I'm surprised our paths haven't crossed."

"Why's that?"

"I lived on the tenth floor of Coleman freshman year—and I'm also starting my senior year at CRU this fall."

Holy shit. It really is a small world. "How long has your nana had a place in Seaside?"

Eyes still wide, she covers her gaping mouth. "My entire life."

Holy, shit. How have we not crossed paths?

"Did you visit often?"

Before she can respond a "Lanie… order's up," comes from the small kitchen window.

Glancing at the food, then back to me, she hesitates.

"Go. It's not like I'm going anywhere. Besides, if you don't put my order in soon, I'm not responsible if I hijack someone else's while I wait."

This makes her laugh. "Alright. Alright. I'm going. We wouldn't want that now."

With that, she turns and I'm left to wonder. *How have I not met her before? There's no way our paths crossed and I simply don't remember her, right?*

Chapter 7
Lanie

AS IF I'M on autopilot, I place Ryan's order and deliver food to my patient customers. I check in on everyone in my section, all the while I can't believe he's been right under my nose the entire time.

Maybe you weren't meant to meet yet?

Do I even believe in fate? I mean, Dad's always drilled that we have to make our own fate, for as long as I can remember. But why are we only meeting now?

After dropping off Ryan's beer, a few more tables fill and I get so busy, I don't get to chat or even stop by his booth again until I'm dropping off his meal.

As I approach he yawns heavily and runs a hand down his face. But the moment I come into his view, his face morphs into a grin. "Wow, that smells delicious," Ryan says as he pats his stomach. "I'm starving."

"Thankfully no other patrons lost their meal in the process. That would've been disastrous."

He chuckles as his eyes roll to the back of his head. "No kidding. Hangry is not pretty on me." Taking a drink of his beer he sighs in appreciation. "Ahhh... this is good. You have no idea what you're missing out on. Are you closing tonight?"

Shaking my head, I shrug. "I'm off at eight. I'm on the early shift tonight. Ben, the owner, had me come in to cover the lunch and dinner rush this week, to get me back in the swing of things."

Cocking his head to the side he asks, "This isn't your first summer?"

"Nope.... started last year. I love working for Ben and couldn't wait for my three-week summer course to be over, so I could return."

"Aren't those summer courses like, all day long?"

A groan escapes my lips before I can stop myself. "Don't remind me. I'm glad to get the class done, but all I did was eat, sleep, and study."

Ryan's lips tip at the edges like he's holding back a smile. "Replace study with work—and you've just described my life at the moment."

"Though summers also mean hanging out with my sisters, so I can't complain."

When the bell above the door chimes with another customer, my attention's drawn to them. Before I leave, Ryan grins and points with the knife in his hand toward the couple looking around. "Go. I've got a steak to enjoy."

"Let me know if you need anything," I offer, then turn and

greet the couple who's walked in the door as Janelle, the other server working tonight, is busy with customers of her own.

What I love most about this job is how quickly time flies. I'm constantly busy with the ebb and flow of patrons. Even on a weekday in a small town like Seaside, we definitely have our regulars who keep our tables filled. But summer brings constant tourists with money to burn as well. The tips alone make it worth my while.

As I work my way around the room checking in on customers, my eyes have a mind of their own and flit to Ryan more than I'd ever admit. Unlike most guys my age, his head isn't in his phone. His phone is face-down on the table and his focus is on the plate in front of him.

The moment he pushes his plate forward and leans his head again on the wall behind him, I flit in his direction hoping our conversation from before continues and I learn more about him. "Are you ready for dessert? We've got a Marionberry pie everyone is raving about."

"Ug, don't I know. I'm not sure what Nell puts in her pies, but they are to die for." Sighing he continues. "Sadly, I don't have any room. What about two pieces to go?"

Two pieces? He must love her pastries. "I'll make that happen."

Then he catches me off guard when he completely changes the subject. "Did you walk to work?"

"Uh..." Why is he asking that? That's odd. Even for him.

When he raises a brow and waits, I go with the truth. "Yeah. I did. But what makes you so interested?"

"You carried a boatload of groceries home with you

yesterday morning, instead of driving. Hmmm...originally I asked out of curiosity, to see if my hunch was right."

"And now?"

"It also gives me an excuse to ask if I can drive you home?"

Cocking my head to the side, I study him carefully. There's not an ounce of uncertainty in his expression. But why would he wait nearly an hour to drive me less than two miles?

When the answers don't come to me, I finally speak the loudest thought aloud. "Why?"

Running a hand down his face, he sighs. "That's a legitimate question. Hell, I'm even asking myself the same thing, if I'm being honest." Slowly he inhales and releases his breath as he shrugs. "But it all comes down to one thing. You intrigue me, Lanie. Even though we've gotten off to a rocky start, I find myself wanting to know you better."

Who knew shooting straight from the hip would slay me?

All the questions whirling around in my mind stop on a dime. I swear the world around me disappears and I can only hear the constant strum of my heart beating through my ears as my stomach does a loopy-loop and free-falls from the sky.

Ryan's jaw tightens the longer he waits for my response.

My throat suddenly feels as dry as the Sahara Desert and my tongue sticks to the roof of my mouth as I roll my lower lip under my teeth and replay his words in my mind.

God, I love his bluntness.

I'm so sick of guys who play games.

Don't even get me started on that five o'clock shadow he's sporting.

He's sexy as sin and from the moment he walked inside the restaurant, I've wanted to run my fingers along his scruff.

"Lanie?" he asks and I remember he's waiting for an answer.

Shit.

"Yes."

"Yes, as in you're finally acknowledging that I've spoken to you? Or are you saying yes to me taking you home?"

God, I'm such a dork.

Shrugging, I smile at my idiocy and I admit, "Both."

Chapter 8
Ryan

"ARE you in a hurry to go home?" I ask as soon as she gets settled into my work truck. Normally, I drive an SUV, but working for Dad this summer, it's easier to drive a company rig.

"Not really," she admits. "Though you're the one with an early schedule. I'm not working until eleven."

"You let me worry about me," I say, shutting her door and running to the other side of the truck to hop in.

The minute I join her in the cab she asks, "Why do I get the feeling you're going to regret that statement? You have to get up early tomorrow."

"I'm not an old geezer who goes to bed before the sun. Can I help it if I'm not ready for my time with you to end?"

"So you say," she mumbles something about wondering why, but I don't quite catch all of it.

That shit won't do in my book.

"Look, I know you're a client. I know shit could go

sideways and it would be a miserable summer for both of us—but what if it doesn't?"

God, she's gonna think I'm nuts. I need to find an explanation that will make sense. To both her and myself at this point.

After a few moments of silence, I lay it all on the line. I've watched from the sidelines for way too long. After watching the one I compared all others to meet someone and truly fall in love, I vowed I wouldn't stand back and let life pass me by again. I'm tired of staying in the safe lane and it's fucking time I stepped up and took a chance on being happy for myself.

But there's no way I can explain this to Lanie—just yet. Maybe when the time is right. But the time isn't today. Realizing she's waiting for me to say more, I blurt out the rest of my conversation from my mind. "Hell, I'm certainly not gonna get into this now, but trust me when I tell you I've wasted way too much time not listening to my gut. With you, there are just too many coincidences to ignore."

"So... I'm not the only one feeling whatever *this* is... that's going on between us?"

"I have no idea where it will lead... but can we start by spending more time together—not because we're forced to—but because you choose to be with me?"

A playful smirk forms on her beautiful face. "Let's start with tonight and go from there."

"Okay, I'll take that. Are you up for heading over to the Point? The tide is out and we can walk along the beach."

"Sure. I can't tell you how many hours I've spent watching my sisters surf from there."

Interesting.

"You don't surf?"

Shaking her head adamantly, she says, "Nope. I prefer to know what's under me when I swim. Besides, I crashed and burned once while I was learning pretty bad. That was all it took for me to view surfing as a spectator sport."

She's freaking adorable.

"That can do it to you," I say with a laugh, but quickly add, "Sorry, you were hurt though," when I realize she might take it the wrong way.

"It was more a hit to the ego and confidence, but I'm just not into drinking the ocean when I crash."

"Yeah, it's not supposed to work that way."

Her light laugh fills the cab of the truck as she spits out, "No kidding."

Once we've made our way down the few rocks between the road and the shore, Lanie stops and takes a seat on one of the bigger rocks. "Don't get me wrong, I love the sand, but it doesn't belong in my work shoes."

Within seconds, she's got her shoes off and is wiggling her toes in the sand. When she doesn't get up right away, I sit beside her on a rock and kick off my own shoes. Unfortunately, I didn't have another pair of boots this morning, so my Romeos had to do. But they're much easier to kick off than work boots, so I can't complain.

Once we start walking she waggles her expressive brows and asks, "So... when you're not working, what do you like to do in Seaside?"

"Hmmm.... When I was younger, I hung out with friends.

But since high school, we've all gone our separate ways and kinda outgrew one another. I hadn't planned on being in town this summer, so I haven't really told anyone I'm back. Lately though I haven't done much but work."

"I can relate. I don't think I talk to many people from high school either, other than a few of my closer friends. Wait... what were your original plans?"

"Let's just say, I originally planned to spend the summer in Boston and it didn't work out."

I watch her chew on her lower lip for a long minute, then she straightens her spine and looks me directly in the eye. "Girl problems?"

"God, no," I spit out in a laugh from her unexpected bluntness. "I know I work for my family company, so I don't have a lot of room to talk, but let's just say nepotism isn't always a good thing for companies."

Her brows knit together and her lips purse. "What do you mean?"

"I went to Boston for an internship. My goal is to get into managing commercial projects on a large scale. I had this awesome opportunity to work for Don Stanford, a bigwig out in Boston, who's taken his small company and is doing the things I would love to learn more about. I've studied his career and admired some of the things he's been involved in."

"So what happened?"

"He's getting close to retirement and wants his son to take over the company... and let's just say we didn't really see eye-to-eye. His son wants to take shortcuts and some could have risked injury. When I brought it up, he used his clout of being the owner's son as his defense for how things would be done on the project. I tried to stick it out a few weeks, but when it became obvious Don was not actually going to be teaching me anything this summer, and one of my co-workers had to file for workman's comp from an unnecessary injury, I quit on the spot. I'm not willing to risk my name or reputation working for a clown that doesn't know his ass from his elbow on a job site."

"Was he hurt bad?"

"No, he only needed a few stitches. But the fact that it happened at all is what pushed me to the breaking point. We'd already worked nearly twelve hours that day and Theo was pushing for us to rush through this one section. In his haste, he left a hammer on the ladder to grab something he needed. Andy thought he was done and went to move the ladder as he'd been instructed and the hammer came off, and it missed his hardhat, but sliced his shoulder on the way down."

"Ohmigod, that's horrible." She gasps.

"Yes. It was. But the worst part is instead of apologizing for leaving it up there to begin with, he ripped into Andy for moving the ladder in the first place. If this had been the first incident. I would have chalked it up to the wrong place, wrong time situation."

Anger courses through me, remembering his response. Calming myself, I take a deep breath. "Let's just say... Theo's management style didn't mesh with mine. He created an extremely hostile work environment."

Lanie shakes her head and mutters, "No one deserves that."

"The first time I had concerns, I tried to handle it myself.

After another week went by and things kept happening, I finally voiced my concerns to the owner. Unfortunately, he dismissed it as… 'well, Theo's still learning the ropes.'"

Lanie groans and rolls her eyes, but I continue. "Yeah, I couldn't agree more. I just couldn't in good conscience stay at a company like that."

"It sounds like you made the right decision."

Rubbing the back of my neck I sigh, relieving all the tension built by just discussing this subject. "I did. Though it sucks that it didn't work out. I really wanted to expand my experience in that area."

"I get it. But maybe it's like that old Garth Brooks song about unanswered prayers?"

"You're a country music fan?"

She stares out at the crashing waves as a slow smile spreads across her face. "It was Nana's favorite. I can't tell you how many times I'd visit and she'd have everything from Patsy Cline, Merle Haggard, and Dolly Parton to the most popular singers today, like Jason Aldean. Honestly, I'm eclectic in my music tastes."

Now I'm curious. "Really, how so?"

"I grew up listening to country with Nana, heavy metal and classic rock with Dad, and Mom was more into top forties, though she would throw in some alternative rock and even R&B, hip hop, and artists like Eminem… so basically, if you turn a radio station to nearly any channel, I'm notorious to singing along with it."

She's so animated as she talks, I'm dying to know more about her. "But do you have a personal preference?"

"Nope. I'm more or less a mood listener. Growing up with three sisters we've always had music on in the house, and trust me, we've each gone through many stages. I guess if I had to choose, it would likely be pop or alternative rock. What about you?"

"Alternative rock and whatever's popular on the radio. Living out here, we don't always have the best reception for streaming and I hate riding in a quiet car for long distances, so I often resort to the radio."

"Will you go to any concerts at the Seaside festival?"

"I hadn't really thought about it. The town's already crazy enough being summer but between the festival and that big movie being filmed, I'm not sure I want to deal with the crowds," I admit.

"Wow, you wake up at the ass crack of dawn and you don't like crowds. Do you also yell at people to stay off your lawn?"

This woman. "Har. Har. I'm not nearly old enough for that. I just like the quiet side of Seaside, when we can get across town in less than ten minutes, versus thirty. I take it you're a fan of the festival?"

"Honestly, I am. I can't wait for it. Not only will I kill it in tips, but I typically get at least one night off to enjoy the festivities. I've already got tickets to the book signing happening. A few of my favorite authors are coming to town. It will be amazing to meet them."

The way she lights up at that last part makes me think there's something more. "Really? Who's that?"

"Ohmigod, two of my favorite authors are coming to this

tiny town. Charlotte Anne *and* Stone Ryder will be in the same place at the same time."

Holy shit. What are the odds?

How the hell do I tell her, without giving up Dani's anonymity? Rubbing my palm down my face, I admit, "I... uh... met Charlotte Anne's brother on campus last year."

"What?" she practically shrieks. "He goes to CRU?"

Fuck. She got it wrong. "No... he's not a student. He's actually dating... I mean, engaged... to my best friend's sister."

"Wow. Have you met Charlotte?"

"Not yet, but I'm sure it's only a matter of time. Since freshman year, Vince has practically become family and I'm attending his twin sister's wedding next month."

"That is so cool. With her being married to Luke Leighton, I'm sure you'll meet him, too."

"I take it you're a Renegades fan as well?"

"How can I not be?" she asks in disbelief. "Though he certainly does make watching the games easy on the eyes."

Did she really just say that?

Cocking a brow in her direction, I ask, "Is this something I should be worried about?"

Lanie swats at my arm. "No, silly. Though I appreciate his beauty, he's happily married and a little out of my age range, don't ya think?"

Somehow my body relaxes and I didn't know just how much her answer would mean. Before I can let myself dwell on that bit of information, I quickly respond. "Hey, no judgment, but it's nice to know I won't need to view him as competition."

"Competition?"

Way to go, doofus. How the hell do you plan to get out of this one?

"Just trying to figure out your type," I admit honestly.

Shit. Lanie's rolling her lower lip under her teeth.

Why the fuck did I say that?

Slowly she exhales and her back straightens, as she pins me with those beautiful blue eyes. Fuck. I'm not sure I want this answer.

My heart's thundering so hard in my chest, it might bruise my ribs.

"So, we're perfectly clear. I'm fairly certain if I had to choose a type..."

Fuck.

Simultaneously, I blurt out, "You don't have to answer that."

As she says, "It would be you, Ryan."

Blinking in surprise, I'm certain I've misheard her.

"C... Come again?" I sputter in disbelief.

I swear my heart is about to take flight out of my chest as I process the words she said.

Cocking her head to the side, she stares at me for an immeasurable amount of time.

Finally, she puts me out of my misery and she utters the words I never thought I'd hear. "You're exactly my type, Ryan."

Chapter 9
Lanie

GREAT. I finally go for broke and barrel out of my comfort zone and he thinks I've fucking lost my mind. He stares at me in disbelief. What the hell have I done?

Mortification doesn't even begin to describe the emotions crashing through me. My abruptness stopped us in our tracks and I don't even have the excuse of walking to preoccupy my thoughts.

Glancing down the beach toward the house, I wonder if I should make a run for it and avoid him like the plague for the rest of the summer. Surely, I can do that, right?

When I feel his large hand reach out and brush a lost strand of hair behind my ear, I'm forced to meet his dark blue eyes. His expression is unreadable and I can't push the air from my chest to breathe.

Taking a step closer, he cups my cheek as he whispers, "Good."

Good? Good what?

The distance between us closes in slow motion as he grins. "Now I can do this."

Before my mind can catch up or hell, even process what he means, his lips connect with mine. For a long moment, I'm so shocked I'm literally frozen in place.

Sliding his hand to the base of my neck, he guides my head to tip up for a better angle, and he kisses me once more.

Just as he's about to pull away, my brain finally wakes the fuck up and my body responds. Dropping my shoes to the sand, I grip hold of his shirt with both my fists, I pull him closer and kiss him back. The moment his tongue slides across my lips, I part for him and he tastes divine.

My legs go weak and I grip his shirt even tighter. I'm no longer sure if I am holding on to keep him close, or if it's for my own balance. He slides his other hand down to the base of my spine to pull me closer.

The moment I know I'm steady on my feet, my hands snake up to his neck. As if he knows what I need, he pulls me flush against him. The warmth of his body feels spectacular against mine.

When he moans, I swear my panties are rendered useless and my clit pulses with need. It's like I've been a dormant volcano and every nerve ending is suddenly awake. I can't get enough.

His scruff feels even better than I imagined as I run my hand along his chiseled jaw. When he breaks our kiss and starts trailing kisses along my jaw to the column of my neck, he hits a spot right behind my ear that makes me want to melt on the spot.

"Oh, Lanie... you're so responsive... you taste amazing.... and your skin's so soft."

The friction of his scruff, the heat of his breath, and the words whispered in my ear make me want to climb his body. "Yes... Ryan... right there..." I murmur, hoping he'll never stop.

When his teeth graze my lobe and he gives it a slight tug, I'm no longer sure my words are coherent. He feels freaking amazing and I don't want this to stop.

Scraping my fingertips into the short hairs at the base of his neck, I moan in satisfaction. When he drags sensual kisses along my jaw back to my mouth, he growls, "You fucking feel incredible."

When his lips meet mine, I kiss him for all I'm worth. It could be minutes, hours, or an eternity because I never want this to end. I've kissed my share of guys, but nothing... I mean, absolutely no one compares to the way Ryan possesses my entire body with only a few strokes of his hand and licks of his tongue.

If our connection is this strong with only a few kisses, I can't even imagine what it would be like with our clothes off. It feels so incredible.

Suddenly, a horn blares in the distance, and Ryan and I break apart panting. Leaning his forehead against mine, we just stare into each other's face until our breaths are less ragged.

Eventually, I notice how bright the sky is behind him. "Check out that sunset," I whisper.

Leaning in, he kisses me once more before reaching for my hand and turning to face the now pink, purple, and dark blue sky. "It's incredible."

Reaching into his pocket with his free hand, he pulls out his phone. "Moments like this are meant to be remembered."

Guiding me to turn my back to the ocean, he pulls me close to his side. Then reaching his long arm out to the side he starts taking photos of the two of us. Just when I think he's done, he leans in to kiss me again.

When he pulls back, his eyes meet mine. "We should probably get back to the truck, or we're going to be walking back in the dark. Can I interest you in some dessert?"

"Is that a euphemism for something?" I tease.

"No. I have two pieces of pie in my truck if you remember. But I do like where your mind went."

Rolling my eyes, I can't believe I forgot. "Well, then, let's go back to my place. That pie is delicious. But I've got something we're missing."

His brows knit together in confusion. "Really, what's that?"

Triumphantly I smile. "I... my friend... have forks."

Leaning in to kiss me once more, he grins. "Could you be any more perfect?"

Surely, it's only because I thought of utensils, right?

Chapter 10

Ryan

ON MY DRIVE back to Lanie's the next morning, my mind rolls on a repeat of our kisses at the beach as well as our make-out session after dessert. Neither of us took things to the next level, but that didn't mean I didn't think about the possibilities in my shower before bed last night and again this morning.

What the fuck is that woman doing to me?

I seriously can't wait until she gets off work tonight to see her again.

Sure, I'll see her before that, but Jared's back in town and will be joining me any minute at the job site. We've got a lot to make up for and I'd rather keep whatever's going on between Lanie and myself between us—for now.

Since I left after midnight last night, I fully expect Lanie to be asleep when I arrive. I told Jared we wouldn't get started until eight today, to respect the deal I'd made with Lanie. He volunteered to swing by and grab coffee for us, so I'm setting up scaffolding and doing what I can with the twenty minutes or so before we can start.

When I reach Lanie's back deck, I'm surprised to find her awake and drinking coffee wrapped in a blanket on a lounger. Her hair is in a messy bun and a beautiful smile spreads across her lips from behind the cup she's drinking. "Hey, Ryan."

"Mornin', beautiful." I grin in return, leaning in to kiss her on the lips. "I thought you'd still be in bed."

"Well, there's this hot guy working on my place. And with the banging and all, I figured I'd enjoy the peace of the morning before the chaos begins."

"Hot guy, eh?"

Giggling, she takes another sip of her coffee. "That's what you caught from that, huh?"

"Of course. It's not every day I'm called hot."

"Oh, please." She swats at the air. "You know better than that."

I pin her with a look that clearly says, "Do I?" and I'm merely rewarded with an eye roll.

Looking in the direction I arrived, she asks, "Is Jared joining you?"

"Should be here any minute."

"Well, then," she huffs. "Get over here and kiss me before I need to go inside and get out of your way."

"You won't hear me argue with that logic." I smirk, pressing my lips to hers. She tastes of coffee and mint and it's all I can do to keep from getting carried away.

When the distinct sound of gravel crunches from the side of the house, I pull away and whisper, "Rain check?"

Her pout is adorable. "If we must. Though it will be nearly twelve hours."

Waggling my brows, I tease, "Good things come to those who wait."

"Way to be all adulty." Leaning in she pecks me once more before standing up from the chair. "I'm going to head in and get something to eat. Can I bring you out anything?"

"Nah," I say, glancing at the driveway, judging how long I have before Jared appears. "I ate at home. But can I steal another kiss?"

Her eyes dart to the side of the house as she grins mischievously. "Is it stealing if given freely?"

After a chaste kiss, the slamming of a door pulls us apart. "Well, Mr. Murdock. That's my cue to let you get to work."

She bops my lips with the tip of her finger then disappears into the house. I'm left staring at the sway of her glorious ass and adjusting my junk before Jared is any the wiser of just how much of an influence this particular client has on me.

It doesn't take long to bring him up to speed with what I've done, as well as what we need to accomplish today. Before I know it, we're ripping off siding and making great progress. With him here, we manage to remove nearly an entire side by lunch. Even though I'm busy, I steal glances of Lanie through the window, and I'm fully aware of when she steps outside to leave for work.

Jared and I work seamlessly to remove the siding with precision and ease. Throughout the day he's caught me up to speed with his brother and I've filled him in on the crappy situation about my job in Boston. We both agree that I've made the right decision.

As we're finishing lunch, Jared stops eating mid-bite and gives me a funny look.

"What?" I ask, wondering if I have something on my face or something.

"There's something different about you."

What the hell is he talking about?

"You've been getting that dopey far-off look on your face— and I wasn't born yesterday. What's going on with you?"

Shrugging, I try to pull it off. "I don't know what you're talking about."

Jared cocks a brow and waits.

When I don't dignify a response, he nods once then says, "Let's try this again... who is she? I've worked with you for the past three summers and I've known you even longer than that. Either you've got *someone* on your mind, or you're busy passing silent but deadly ones over there." Then the asshole reaches into his pocket and hands over some TUMS. "Here, I think you may need these more than I do."

What the actual fuck?

"No thanks, old man. My gut health is just fine."

"Then what's goin' on?"

There's no way in hell I'm talking with Jared about Lanie. First, it's incredibly new. Who knows if it'll last. So of course, I do what I can to evade the subject entirely by shrugging it off. "Can't a guy just be in a good mood?"

Shaking his head, it's obvious he doesn't believe me, but thankfully he lets it go. "Okay... whatever you say, man. Are you ready to knock off this last side of the house?" With that our lunch break is officially over, and we bust ass to get as much done as we can before quitting time.

Freshly showered, I walk through the door of Pop's. I'm looking forward to seeing the girl that hasn't been far from my mind all day. The moment she spots me, her face lights up with the most beautiful smile and I'd be lying if that doesn't make my chest swell. She closes the distance between us with a cheerful greeting, "Hey, Ryan."

When she stops in front of me and hesitates, it takes everything in me not to lean in and kiss her. But she's working, so I can't. Instead, I ask, "How was your day?"

A light laugh escapes as she looks around the crowded bar. "Busy. But that's how I like it. Have you eaten?"

"No, but if you're hungry, I'd rather wait and eat with you."

"I'm starving, but I've got about twenty more minutes before my shift is over. Can I get you something to drink while you wait?"

"A Coke sounds great. Wanna eat here or somewhere else?"

Looking around the room she shrugs. "Here is fine," she says as she walks me to a booth nearby. "If you let me know what your order is, I'll put both of ours in before I get off, so we don't have to wait. I skipped lunch and I'm starving."

"Why'd you do a thing like that?"

"I wasn't hungry on my break because I'd eaten a big breakfast. I figured I'd grab something on my next one as I usually get another break during a lull. However, we've been slammed since I returned, and obviously, that never happened."

When another customer walks through the door, I quickly offer, "Don't let me get in the way. I'm good just resting for a minute myself."

She nods and flits to wait on the next customer. I find myself watching her move around the room until she goes to the back for something. That's when I decide I'd rather not be a creeper. So, I pull out my phone and get up to date with my social media feeds as a distraction.

Eventually, she comes back with my Coke and takes my order. The moment she leaves, I make a mental note that our next date will *not* be here. Don't get me wrong, this is a great place, but she deserves being catered to, not waiting on herself.

She proves my point when she eventually returns with two large plates piled with food. Instead of dropping them off at another table, she sets them on mine.

"Whew... I'm starving," she mutters when she plops down across from me.

"Next time we go out, it'll be a proper date," I mutter, though I'm not sure if it's a message for myself or a warning to her.

"Next time?" She raises a brow and a playful smile rolls across her lips. "What makes you so sure of yourself?" Then she shakes her head before tacking on, "And just how old are you? Who uses a word like proper?"

Oh, that little brat. The heated look in her eyes as they trace my lips, then back to mine. She knows good and well, what I mean.

Clearing my throat, I lean forward with my arms on the table. "If I wasn't clear last night, I'll rectify that now." I pause and wait for her full attention. "I like you, Lanie. I want to see more of you. I love hanging out with you, but I want to take you on a *proper* date—you know one where we *both* get waited on. One where you relax and are spoiled as well."

Shrugging, she grabs a steak fry and plops it in her mouth. "This is still a date. It doesn't matter who brings out the food."

Shaking my head, I mutter, "Not the point."

She raises a brow in challenge. "Do *you* consider this a date?"

"Any time I spend with you is considered a date," I admit. "The point I clearly didn't make, is that I want you to know I'm not being lazy and actually put effort into planning our time together."

Rolling her eyes, she chomps on another fry. "Okay... but for the record, I don't need grandiose plans or anything fancy. In fact, I prefer low-key dates with quality time to extravagant outings."

"Same. But that doesn't mean I won't take you places where you can be spoiled, too. Heck, if you're lucky, I may even cook for you."

"Oh, now that's something I can't wait to see."

Grabbing a fry of my own, I tease, "Be careful what you wish for."

I'm a decent cook. In fact, I think I'm pretty good. I have to be if I want anything other than takeout or microwaved meals. But I don't want her expectations higher than I can meet.

As we finish our burger and fries, she tells me about her

day, and I fill her in on the progress of her home. I truly don't think I've enjoyed spending time with anyone like this in forever. She makes me laugh and I feel so at ease with her.

When another waitress stops in to check on us, I order two pieces of pie to go. As soon as she leaves, Lanie asks, "Do you have a secret pie addiction or something?"

"Nope. I just know what I like, so why settle for less? Besides, last night I shared it with this amazing girl on our first date. It brought me luck and I'm not about to change things up."

This earns me another laugh. "Hmmm.... So many things can be taken from that statement."

Replaying my words in my head I realize there are so many truths. Unapologetically, I smirk with a challenge, "Take it as you wish."

Chapter 11
Lanie

THIS GUY... from the moment he arrived at Pop's, he's kept me on my toes. Sometimes he's a bit cocky, other times completely humble. One thing is certain, I'm really starting to like him. He makes me feel like I'm the only one in the room and when he smiles... I feel it deep in my core.

Right now, at this very moment, he's waiting patiently for me to take a quick shower and change. I had someone spill their drink on me early in my shift and I've felt sticky all day. We've decided to come back to my place to watch a movie. But now as I stare at myself in the mirror, I'm left with a major dilemma... look cute or get comfy?

I've already taken off what little makeup I wear, and I won't be refreshing it—especially if it means I keep him waiting longer. But do I put on leggings? Or stick with shorts and a t-shirt?

He did say this was a date, so maybe I should put some effort into things.

Okay... shorts it is.

Quickly, I slide them up my legs and throw on a t-shirt. My hair's still wet, but that will just have to do. It's not like we're going anywhere. I take the few necessary minutes to run a brush through my hair, then rush downstairs.

When I approach, I'm happy to see he's made himself at home. He took his shoes off at the door, so his large feet are propped up on the ottoman and his head is resting against the back of the couch. He's got the TV on and he's completely immersed in the recap of a baseball game from earlier this evening.

The moment he spots me, he mutes the television and sits forward. "Feel better?"

"Much." I sigh in relief. "Are you hungry? Do you want any snacks for the movie?"

Patting the seat beside him, he says, "I'm stuffed. Here, come put your feet up. You've had a long day and I'm sure you could use the rest."

"I'm gonna grab myself some iced tea, want some? I have that, wine, or water. I need to make a trip to Costco before my sisters come to stock up on things."

Standing to join me in the kitchen he asks, "When do they get here?"

"The twins will be here this weekend. Then next Thursday we leave for Lizzy's graduation in Tacoma. That reminds me—that Sunday. We should be able to host a party here, right? Dad wants me to make sure we'll have access to the deck for the grad party."

Nodding in understanding, Ryan smiles. "I can make that happen. I'm not sure where we'll be with the siding or the roof, but now that we've been warned, we'll do our best to make it functional for you."

So relieved everything is working out, I throw my arms around his neck and hug him fiercely. "Thanks. This is the first big event we've had since Nana's funeral and I'm determined to make it a success."

"Just let me know what you need, and I'll do what I can to make it happen."

When he pulls me in closer for a hug, I completely sink into him. I had no idea just how much I needed this... and God, Ryan gives the best hugs. He'll never know just how much this small gesture means to me.

Sometimes I feel like I've got my shit together, other times I have no idea just how fragile my emotions are until I'm smacked in the face by the smallest act of kindness. In order to get through the days since losing Nana, I've just kept placing one foot forward and didn't let myself focus on anything but the task at hand.

His strong arms hold me close and his masculine scent washes over me. Inhaling deeply, I enjoy his warmth as it sinks into me and his steady heartbeat calms me. As if he can sense my need, he squeezes harder and I sigh, "Thanks."

I'm not sure how long we stand like this, but eventually he pulls his head back to look me in the eyes. "You good?"

"Yeah," I sigh. "I needed that."

A sly grin tips his lips. "Any time... now tell me about these sisters. Just how many do you have?"

"Three. Raven and Sloane are twins. They just turned nineteen and are both attending Gonzaga. Lizzy is the youngest. She's graduating from high school and turns eighteen next month."

"Wow... and you're how old?"

"I turned twenty-one in April... I know my parents were crazy to have four of us in less than five years."

"I only have one sister, Jessica. She graduated last year and is working on her nursing degree at Wazzu."

"Is she at Pullman or one of the branch campuses?" I ask, knowing he means Washington State University.

"Pullman. She'll be in Spokane eventually. She's staying on campus this summer and won't visit until August—if she even bothers to come home."

"I can't imagine not spending a summer with my sisters," I admit. "Even after I become a teacher, I hope we can still do this—at least until we're all out of school."

"What grades do you want to teach?"

"I think I wanna teach middle school. I've done some internships at both the elementary and middle school levels and I love that age."

"Uh... when I look back at middle school, I could've sworn we were just a bunch of hormonal jerks who thought we knew everything."

"Ha..." I laugh. "You're right. But they're also the most challenging students to reach. I love finding ways to make connections and helping students be the best they can be.

Sure, their frontal lobes haven't fully developed, so they aren't always thinking clearly, but I love the content at that level. I love math and that is one of the most fundamental ages to influence. I've had both good and bad math teachers, trust me. But I think I can make a difference. My endorsement will allow me to teach both middle school and high school. But enough about me. Have you decided what movie we're watching?"

Shaking his head, he replies. "I'm game with anything."

"Really? If you're up to it, Charlotte Anne's latest romantic suspense just came out on Passionflix and I've been dying to see it."

"Will it matter if I haven't read the books?"

"From what I've been told—no. Though I'm sure the book is better."

"Okay, then, let's get settled on the couch and you can introduce me to one of your favorite author's works."

Oh, my heart.

His eagerness at watching something I'm passionate about makes my chest tighten and my belly flit with thousands of butterflies. If I wasn't already falling, this would definitely be cause.

Reaching up on my tiptoes, I pull his face to mine and kiss him quickly. The moment our lips touch I know I could easily get lost in him. However, he must sense the same thing because, after all too short of a time, he breaks our kiss.

Leaning his head toward the living room, he says, "Don't get me wrong, I'm *all* for kissing you, but I think we'd better go watch the movie before things get carried away."

"Would that really be a bad thing?"

Ryan growls and steps away from me completely. "Oh, Lanie, what am I gonna do with you?"

Just about anything you want. My inner vixen screams, but I'm fairly certain he meant that as a rhetorical question—so I playfully wink then turn and grab a glass from the cupboard.

Within a few minutes, the movie's cued up and we're settled on the couch. I'm snuggled into his side and his arm drapes over my shoulder. It takes a few minutes for my body to relax. Between that kiss, his delicious scent, and the promise of more, I'm no longer sure the movie will hold my interest. But his steadying breaths settle me and shortly after the opening credits roll, the plot pulls me into the storyline I've been obsessed with for years.

Eventually, I'm so sucked into the movie, my heart races as the characters struggle with their first major dilemma. Hell, I even flinch when the other shoe drops, and they're left in despair.

When Ryan notices, he chuckles. "Don't you know what's coming next?"

"Yes, but I feel the same way when I re-read the books, too. I get so lost in the moment, I forget what's coming next."

"I wish I could do that," Ryan grumbles. "I don't think I've ever re-read a book on purpose, once I started reading chapter books."

Leaning forward, I stare into his eyes in disbelief. "Really?"

His chin pulls back to his chest as the "What?" flies out of his mouth, clearly in defense mode.

"You've never re-read a book?"

Rubbing a finger down the bridge of his nose, he shakes his head. "I know what happened, so what's the point?"

"But don't you ever just want to feel the emotions of the book again? Like being transported back into that world and getting lost?"

"Uh... all I have to do is read the title or be reminded of it and I remember it all."

"That's just... weird," I admit when nothing else comes to mind.

He has the gall to chuckle. "Tell me how you really feel, why don't you."

"Does that work for everything? Or just things you read?"

"Oh, I've been known to forget things... trust me. Like I'll know something is happening on the twelfth but won't actually realize that the twelfth is tomorrow if that makes sense. But mainly just things I read."

"I'll bet that comes in handy for school," I grumble, wishing I only had to read things once.

"It has its perks." He shrugs. Then points to the TV. "Are we gonna find out if their plan works? Or do you want to turn it off? I'm kinda invested and need to know how they take down this terrorist. I already know it will have an HEA, as it's a romance. But I wanna know how they take those bastards down."

"HEA? You're speaking my language."

"Hey, everyone deserves their own Happily Ever After, don't ya think?"

On instinct, I poke him in the chest.

"Hey, what was that for?" He peers down at me confused.

"Just checkin' to see if you're for real."

Before I can pull away, he grabs my wrist and pulls me close to him. When we're only a breath away from each other, he whispers, "I'm very real. Flaws and all." Leaning in, he kisses me chastely then maneuvers me so that I'm back in my original position beside him.

I'm sure my expression remains confused because my mind's reeling from his abruptness.

"Don't worry, sweet girl. There's plenty more where that came from. But let's finish the movie first."

Hmmm... I'm not quite sure what to make of bossy Ryan.

Chapter 12
Ryan

WHAT IN THE *hell has gotten into me?*

First, I'm telling her about my photographic memory. Then the next thing I know, I'm manhandling her like one of the characters in the movie we're watching.

I seriously can't believe I did that.

But from the heat in her eyes, it's obvious she didn't hate it.

I wasn't lying when I said I'm invested and need to know how the movie ends. But the real reason is I'm not ready to rush into things. It feels like I've known her forever, but in reality, it's literally been two days. A point I keep reminding myself because Lanie's the sexiest woman I've ever laid eyes on —and she has no clue what she does to me.

It's not that I'm opposed to one-night stands, but with her, there's a possibility of more. I've only felt this way once in my life and I fucked it up by sitting on the sidelines. I certainly won't make that mistake again. But with Lanie... even after two days, I know I need to play the long game and tread carefully. She's also been through a lot with her grandma's passing. I don't want to ruin things by moving too fast.

Eventually, I stop thinking about the woman in my arms and return my focus to the movie. It's not my typical first pick, but honestly, I think I'd enjoy reading the book, though this movie is pretty fantastic on its own.

When the movie ends, I'm surprised Lanie doesn't move. I figured she'd be chomping at the bit demanding to know what I thought of it. She'd been so eager to know my thoughts earlier and it practically killed her to keep from spoiling it for me. But she managed. When I look down, I'm surprised to find her sound asleep against my chest.

I can't help but admire her beauty. For the first time, I notice the natural highlights around her face and a light sprinkling of freckles across her nose and the top of her cheeks. Her lashes are long and thick. God, she's absolutely breathtaking. She's so peaceful, I don't have the heart to wake her. Reaching for the remote, I select another movie to watch and settle in to just snuggle her.

While I'm waiting for it to begin, I spot a blanket on her side of the couch. In a snap decision, I snag it and do my best to cover her with one hand. The moment she's covered, I feel her burrow deeper against me. When the opening credits of the latest Marvel movie begin, I rest my head against the back of the couch.

I could get used to having Lanie in my arms.

The next thing I know, the loud beep... beep... beeeeeepppp of my alarm jolts me awake. Keeping my eyes closed because I'm just not ready to start the day, I reach for it on my bedside, but all I get is a hand full of hair.

Hair? What the fuck is going on?

As if someone reads my mind, "Make it stop…" is moaned and something pats at my leg.

My eyes bolt open and I'm blinded by the light coming into the room. Eventually they focus and I am suddenly very aware of my surroundings. "Fuck. I fell asleep." I grapple along the couch to where my phone's still beeping, getting louder with each long pause.

Eventually, I find it wedged between Lanie and the couch cushion. When I finally turn off the alarm, I glance at the clock and realize I'm screwed. I have less than forty minutes to drive home, change, and return.

However, Lanie's still a lead weight wrapped against me. Somehow, I'm hunched over on my side, and her head's resting on my lower abdomen. I have no idea how we ended up in this position, but if I move without waking her, she'll end up being dumped on the floor.

Using the hand that's been resting against her hip, I shake her gently. "Lanie… Lanie. I need you to wake up."

"Five more minutes," she mumbles and reaches for the blanket that's been pushed around her hips.

"Sorry, sweet girl. I can't do that. I've gotta haul ass to get home as it is to get back here on time. I need you to let me up. Lanie? Did ya hear me?"

When I shake her again, her soft and languid body instantly stiffens, her eyes bolt open, and she looks around the room. "Wha... what's goin' on?" comes out groggy and confused.

Shrugging, I smile apologetically. "Sorry. I guess I fell asleep. Do you think you can let me up so I can get to work on time?"

A playful smirk plays around her lips. "But you're already here," she reminds me.

"Yes, but my work clothes aren't. Jared will be here soon and I'd rather not be late."

She pushes away from my lap to sit up and nearly falls off the couch. Thankfully, I'm able to catch her. "Whoa. Slow down. I don't wanna hurt you."

When she finds her balance, she mutters, "I'm good. I'm so sorry I fell asleep. Did you at least finish the show?"

"Yeah. It was great. You may have convinced me to read the series, if there are more books about the other characters."

Grinning triumphantly, she pats me on the chest. "I told you it's an amazing series. I've got them all on e-book if you want me to loan them to you."

"Not to be rude, but I really gotta get moving. Can we rain check this conversation?" When she doesn't say anything, I quickly tack on. "What about tonight when you get off? I can pick you up again."

"Uh, today's my day off, so I'm sticking around the house."

"Mind if I stop in when I'm done workin'?"

"Only if you'll let me cook you dinner? I've been craving one of Nana's casseroles and it's way too much for me to make for only myself."

"It's a date," I say, leaning in to kiss her cheek. "Good morning, by the way."

"Good morning," she says, suddenly shy, then she mumbles, "How is it you look even better with your messy hair and shadow of scruff? That's just not fair. I probably look like Medusa and you're like a Greek God or something."

"Ha..." I chortle. "You're hysterical in the morning. But for the record, I think you're gorgeous any time of day."

"You sure know how to boost a girl's ego."

But I never want her questioning herself, especially where I'm concerned. So I pointedly remind her, "Eventually, you'll realize I rarely say anything I don't mean."

For the longest time, she stares at me and just blinks.

When I notice the clock behind her, I panic. I have less than thirty minutes. "Look. Sorry to rush out, but I gotta go."

Pushing me toward the door, she says through her laughter, "Go... stop being all cute and distracting... and get out of here."

Chapter 13
Lanie

RYAN WORKING RIGHT outside my house has been more of a distraction than I would've thought. Having contractors in general banging on the house is bad enough. But it's taking every ounce of self-control I have, not to seat myself in the living room and do nothing but watch him throughout the day.

It's pathetic. I know. I even went so far as prepping the entire meal for tonight—before noon—simply so I had the excuse of being downstairs. Just as I'm setting the casserole in the fridge for later, there's a knock at the front door.

Wondering who it could be, I rush to answer it.

Knowing the guys are right out back if I need them, I don't even bother to check before swinging it open, only to be frozen in place.

The sight of Ryan lifting the hem of his shirt to wipe off his face is a sight to be seen. He's fit, not in an *I'm a gym buff*, but I *work my ass off* kind of way. The navy shirt he's wearing matches his expressive eyes and his chiseled jaw still has a day's growth of beard from yesterday. The minute his eyes meet mine his lips tip into a hypnotic grin.

This man is something alright.

Eventually, my brain kicks in and I remember how to form words.

"Well, you're certainly not a solicitor."

Shrugging, he muses, "True... but I did come to sell you on something."

"Something you couldn't have come to the back door for?"

His lips quirk into a playful smirk. "Well, what would be the fun in that?"

"Hmmm..." I ponder, wondering where he's going with this.

"Jared's on his way to grab some materials and I've got about forty minutes for lunch. Since I didn't have time to make one this morning, can I tempt you into running to town and grabbing something with me?"

"I've got one better," I counter. "Unless you've got a hankering for somethin' special, why don't you come in and I'll fix us some lunch? After all, I'm the reason you were running late this morning.

"I've already got bacon cooked and I was gonna offer you a BLT—but you've beaten me to it."

Reaching for my hip, he pulls me to him as he whispers, "I guess great minds think alike."

"Really? Cuz all I can think about is kissing you..." I playfully grab his t-shirt and pull him closer.

He steps inside and swings the door shut behind him and growls, "Again... same page," right before his lips crash onto mine.

Tipping up on my toes, I pull myself closer as his large hand runs along my spine and pins me in place. Between hot languid kisses that light me from the inside out, he once again reads my mind as he pants, "You... have... no idea... how much I... needed this."

You and me both. It's like my best fantasies throughout the morning have come to life. With every nip, suck, and breath between us, my need for him grows. When my teeth pluck on his lower lip, he responds by gripping my ass with both his hands and hoisting me in the air to meet his height entirely.

On instinct, I cling to him like a velcro monkey by looping my arms around his neck and my legs around his waist. Ryan's scent is intoxicating. It's a mix of fresh ocean air, his seductive cologne, and a hint of sawdust. I seriously can't get enough. I get so caught up in our kisses, I'm caught off guard when I feel my ass land on something solid.

"What the..." I start, but I'm cut off by Ryan's phone ringing.

Kissing me quickly Ryan mutters, "Hold that thought," as he brings the phone to his ear. "Hey, Jared, what's up?"

There's talking from the other end of the line, but I can't quite make out the words. Ryan shakes his head and smiles directly at me and waggles his brow. "No, man. I'm good. I'll grab a bite here."

My eyes dart to his lower lip and I certainly know what I'd like to bite.

However, Ryan interrupts my musing when he nods and says, "No worries. Take your time. I'll see you in a few." Sighing he hangs up the phone. "He's on his way."

His pout is pathetically adorable and I can't help but laugh. "You say that like it's a bad thing. Aren't you fighting the weather to get the siding done as it is?"

"As the foreman of this crew, I should agree with you. As a man who is thoroughly enjoying his lunch break—I'm not ready for it to end."

"Neither am I," I whisper, wrapping my arms around his neck and pulling him closer for a quick kiss. Before we get carried away, I push him back and hop off the counter. "But… you need to eat. Grab a seat at the bar and let's eat lunch together."

"Mind if I use your restroom first?"

Pointing to the hall, I say. "It's the next door after the laundry room."

While he's gone I make quick work and throw together three sandwiches. I grab a bag of barbecue chips from the pantry and I'm just about to slice up the cantaloupe when two arms snake around me from behind.

Leaning in to kiss the side of my neck, he whispers, "You didn't have to go to such trouble."

And he just found my kryptonite.

There's something about being held from behind while whispering in my ear that turns me on like no other. Add kissing me at the base of my neck, and it's the trifecta that turns my thoughts to goo. My nerve endings tingle from my head to my toes as warmth spreads throughout my body. I swear if he keeps talking in that sexy tone, I'll do almost anything he asks.

Please don't stop.

When he pulls away, the synapses in my brain finally connect, and I remember that I should respond. "I was making it for myself and I've got plenty to share."

Reaching into the cupboard I point him towards, Ryan grabs two glasses. "Water or tea?"

His simple gesture reminds me of Nana and I laugh. When his expression turns quizzical, I quickly explain, "Nana had a rule in this house that she'd explain to guests. She always knew how to make a person feel at home. But if you came to visit, she'd bluntly tell you, *'You're only a guest the first time. If you return, you're expected to pitch in—just like anybody else because we won't be waitin' on ya.'* God, I miss her. She may be gone, but she's definitely still here, ya know?"

"She sounds like a wise woman."

"Don't get me wrong; she was the most hospitable woman you'd ever met, but she didn't want you going without because you were afraid to ask for it. She'd rather you just make yourself at home because as Nana would say, she was good at many things—but mind readin' wasn't one of them."

"I wish I had known her. The more I learn, the more I like," Ryan says before taking a bite of his BLT.

My chest tightens at just how much I miss her, but somehow talking about her with Ryan makes me feel happy, too. Gah... Grief is a fickle beast. You never know when it will hit, or how it will impact you. It lingers on the edge between happy and sad memories and I never know how I'll respond.

"I think she would've liked you," I admit.

In my short time with Ryan, I've seen him smirk, I've seen his playful side, but this smile that spreads across his face is genuine and could almost be described as humble. When he whispers, "Thank you. That means a lot." I just want to hug him.

Instead, I change the subject because I'm not taking chances on my emotions at the moment. "Did you live close to your grandparents?"

Finishing another bite, he nods. "My dad's parents live about an hour from here down the coast, and my mom's parents live outside of Salem."

"Do you see them often?"

"Now that we're older, mostly for holidays and birthdays. But when we were younger, we spent a week or so in the summer, at each of their homes. I'm sure it was so my parents could work."

"Same... though Nana watched us during Dad's designated visitation. He was usually stationed somewhere around the world and would request leave to be with us as much as he could." Ryan grabs a chip from his plate as he asks, "What branch of the military?"

"He's still in the Air Force. Right now, he's stationed at Lewis-McChord. He could have retired last year, but I can't see him retiring any time soon."

"Wow. That's really commendable. Is he a pilot?"

"Yes, he's actually a pararescue pilot. That's why he's been stationed all over the world. If he chooses to stay in, he'll likely end up in Germany with his next orders."

"Did you move around a lot growing up?"

"For the first five years of my life—yes. But after my parents divorced, Mom moved us to live near her family at University Place."

"Does your mom still live there?"

Shaking my head, I continue, "No. When Dad got his last assignment, an opportunity for her to become a traveling nurse landed in her lap and Lizzy moved in with him."

When we hear the engine of Jared's truck, Ryan leans closer to me and says, "That's my cue... I can't wait for this day to be over so I can spend more time with you."

With that, he kisses me quickly, then stands to take his plate to the sink.

"Just put them in the sink. I'll take care of it in a minute," I offer, bringing my own dish to join his.

When he's halfway through the sliding glass door to the deck, he stops to face me. "Thanks again for lunch. I'm looking forward to tonight." With that, he shuts the door and walks across the deck out of sight.

He has no idea how much I'm looking forward to seeing him this evening.

I spend the necessary time cleaning up the kitchen before heading up to my room to read. With the constant banging against the wall, I groan in frustration. There's no way I can read under these conditions.

Grabbing my e-reader, I slip on my flip-flops and head downstairs. Stopping in the guest bathroom, I apply sunscreen and grab the large beach blanket that's stored in the linen closet. Then I grab my favorite folding chair from the garage and some snacks before heading to my second favorite place in Seaside—the beach.

Chapter 14
Ryan

WHILE JARED FINISHES the last few things today, I fill out my paperwork and check in with Dad to update him on today's progress. As I listen to him drone on about the progress of a remodel he's doing in Long Beach, my thoughts return to Lanie. I can't wait to spend more time with her tonight. It's like each minute took an hour to pass. I can't wait to finish my day, so I can spend the evening with her. It's been hell, attempting to go through the motions of my typical work day.

Finally, when I see Jared heading this way, I make an excuse to end the call with my dad. "Hey, Dad, Jared's about to leave. I'd better get going."

"Okay, Son. I'll talk with you tomorrow."

Jared walks to his truck as if he's purposely trying to torture me—slow and without a care in the world. He takes his sweet time putting each of his personal tools in his cargo box. Is he gonna pull out a label maker and color code them, too?

Jesus Christ, man. Just get in your friggin' truck and leave.

Nope—I can't be that lucky. The bastard has to pull out his phone and do something with it before even turning over the engine. Finally, he puts his truck in gear and starts rolling down the road.

When his rig is finally out of sight, I grab the bag I'd hastily packed when I ran home this morning. There's no way I wanted to waste more time by driving across town before my date tonight. Before I can exit the vehicle, Lanie's walking down the steps from the back deck and rounding the corner of the house.

The moment her eyes meet mine, a heart-stopping smile spreads across her face. My chest tightens and apparently, I turn into all thumbs, getting out. Thankfully, she's none the wiser of the fact that I nearly fall out of my truck when my toe catches on the bottom lip of the doorjamb.

Could I look any less graceful?

Rocking back on her heels, she pulls her lower lip under her teeth. "I wasn't sure what the plan was. Ready to come inside, or do you need to finish your day first?"

My eyes dart to the bag in the front seat. "If you don't mind me changing here, I'd rather stay."

Her eyes roam over me from head to toe. "Yesterday, I noticed you'd showered after work. I've got plenty of towels and hot water if you wanna use it."

Only if you join me, almost rolls off my tongue, but somehow, I manage to keep that thought to myself. Instead, I merely nod and agree. "I'll just be a few minutes."

Smiling she reaches for my hand. "Well, we've got about

thirty minutes until dinner's ready, so take your time." With that, she leads me inside and shows me which bathroom to use. Wasting no time, as soon as I'm alone, I shuck off my clothes and take the fastest shower humanly possible. It's like I can't get back to her fast enough.

As I descend the stairs, my mouth waters the moment I smell the delicious aroma of Lanie's cooking. When I enter the kitchen, the cheesy casserole is on the stove, and on the counter is more cantaloupe from this afternoon along with a salad. But as I look around the room, Lanie's nowhere to be found.

Confused, I call out, "Lanie?"

A second later, she appears in the hall. "Just grabbing the growler from the fridge in the garage."

When I see Pop's logo, I grin. "Decided to try the Puckering Pear, I see. Is that where you wandered off to today?"

"Yeah, I ended up near Pop's, and I thought I'd give it a try."

"What can I do to help with dinner?"

"If you want to open this, I'll grab us some glasses and plates to dish up."

"It smells amazing. Thanks again for cooking."

Effortlessly, we move around the kitchen plating our food and filling our glasses.

When she sits at the bar, I follow suit. "So what else did you do today?"

Sighing, she looks to the ceiling. "Let's see... after getting some beach therapy, I dropped off my things and went for a walk. When I got back, I talked on the phone with my sister Raven. I guess their plan is to arrive Friday, and both she and Sloane are scheduled to work this weekend."

"They already have jobs lined up?" I ask in surprise.

"Yeah, they each have worked them the last couple of summers. Raven's working at the ropes course here in town and Sloane's a waitress at the Seaside Hotel."

"What about Lizzy?"

"She'll work at a local book shop. Nana set her up with the job last summer and since it's slow in the winter, the owner's looking forward to having her back this summer."

Taking a bite of the chicken casserole, I moan as the savory flavor melts in my mouth. "Mmmm... I think I'm in heaven." I'm not sure what I expected, but I wasn't prepared for the cheesy combination of corn, broccoli, and mushrooms.

"Can you see why I don't like to make it just for myself? I'd eat the entire pan."

"You'll certainly have some competition. I'll definitely be having seconds," I warn as I fork another piece of chicken into my mouth.

"Good," she says with a laugh. "Nana always had the best recipes."

"For the record, if you want to test any others, I'll gladly volunteer to help you eat them." Taking another bite, I muse at its perfection. "Damn. This puts any casserole my mom has ever made to shame—though, don't tell her that."

Smiling, she offers, "Don't worry, your secret's safe with me."

"Mmmmm.... this is good," Lanie says after trying the Puckering Pear.

"I told ya." I grin before taking another bite. "It's one of my favorites."

For a few moments, the room fills with comfortable silence as we devour the food she's prepared. Eventually, we make small talk. I tell her how the siding is coming along on the house and she fills me in on other recipes her nana made that she'd like to try. If any of them are half as delicious as this meal, I'm eager to taste them. Of course, I dish us each up seconds, as I'd predicted, and we continue our casual conversation.

When I can't eat another bite, I push my plate away and ask, "Wanna clean up, then go for a walk?"

"God, I'm stuffed. My eyes are always bigger than my stomach when I eat this. Of course, it tastes so good, so I don't notice until I've completely overindulged."

"I see we have another thing in common." I grin as I stand and take her plate to the sink to rinse it off. "Dishwasher clean or dirty?"

"Uh..." She stares at me for a second too long then says, "Dirty."

"What's that look for?" I finally ask when she's still looking at me as if I've grown two heads.

Shaking her head, she mutters, "Just trying to see if you're real."

What the hell is she talking about? "Why wouldn't I be?" I ask, reaching for the empty fruit bowl.

"Mmmm..." She purses her lips together as if she's

contemplating her words for a response. Then she suddenly shrugs. "You're doing dishes."

"Well, last I checked, you cooked. I ate, I can help clean up. It's not like I'm a neanderthal that doesn't know how to fend for himself. You'll be shocked... I even do laundry, know how to clean toilets, and run a vacuum, too."

She feigns fanning herself as if she might faint. "Now you're just teasing me."

Drying off my hands, I stalk over to where she's now standing in front of the stove and place both hands on the counter at each of her sides, effectively pinning her in place. "Oh, I'm more than just a tease, trust me." I rasp out much sultrier than I intend, as I slant my lips over hers.

Cocking a brow in challenge, she smirks. "Are you sure about that?"

My voice is gravelly when I rasp out, "What do *you* think?"

Fisting my shirt, she pulls me closer and my mouth crashes onto hers. When her tongue sweeps across my lips, they part with ease to let her in and all time ceases to exist. All that matters is how good she tastes, her soft skin, and how this simple kiss completely consumes me. The way her hands glide through my hair at the base of my neck, and her soft body presses against mine, makes my semi-hard dick turn to steel.

Needing more, I break our kiss and trail my lips along her jaw to that place I've quickly learned she loves behind her ear. "God, you feel amazing," I groan as my fingertips slip under the back of her shirt and run along her spine.

When a dog suddenly barks as a child screams "Get back here," Lanie and I freeze in place.

Peering around me, she looks at the path people walk along the promenade, between the house and the beach. An entire family lingers just outside the fence and another sits on a bench nearby.

Reaching for my hand, Lanie jerks me in the direction of the stairs as she whisper-shouts. "Follow me."

"Why are you whispering?" I ask, amused by the pleading look on her face.

As if the people outside could possibly hear her she continues to whisper-shout, "As much as I love this place, I hate the fact that it can also be a fishbowl when the blinds are up."

"Want me to close them?" I offer.

"No," she hisses. "That'll draw too much attention. I've got a better idea."

Tugging on my arm again, I give in and follow. "Okay, but what's your rush?" I ask through laughter at the ridiculousness of this entire situation. I'm not an exhibitionist, but I still don't get why she's in such a hurry.

"I'm not done kissing you," she hisses as if she's annoyed and I should've read her mind.

Her bluntness makes me laugh.

Yeah, I can get on board with that.

"Neither was I," I murmur.

Taking a right at the top of the stairs, she pulls me into a room that faces the ocean. Without saying a word, she reaches behind the sheer curtains to close the wooden blinds.

The moment she's done she turns with a mischievous grin spread across her face as she loops her hands around my neck. "Now... where were we?"

Pulling her closer, I play along, "Hmmmm... I think we were right about... here..." is the last words I mutter before crashing my lips onto hers.

If I thought our kiss downstairs was consuming, I was wrong. There's a sense of urgency that wasn't there before. When my tongue slides in to meet hers, she releases a breathy moan, and all sense of thought disappears as my other senses kick in.

Running my fingers along the hem of her shirt, her soft skin is inviting. She smells like a mixture of fresh ocean breeze with a hint of vanilla and lavender. I feel like I need to taste her everywhere.

Her hands roam my chest, shoulders, and back. She pulls on my shirt as she breaks our kiss and pants, "This needs to go. I wanna feel your skin."

Not needing to be told twice, I step back and rip my shirt over my head in one move. The moment I'm standing before her shirtless, her eyes heat as they roam over me. Before I can close the distance between us, she crosses her arms over her body, grabs the hem of her shirt, and tosses it to the floor.

Between Lanie's bold expression and the way her chest rises and falls with each heavy breath she takes, I nearly forget how to breathe. Her skin looks soft and inviting and she has curves that make my wildest fantasies of what she'd look like pale in comparison. "You're so beautiful," escapes without conscious thought.

Her lips quirk and her eyes heat as her tongue runs along her lower lip. I can feel every inch of her eyes roaming over me from head to toe. Her smile turns wicked when she whispers, "You're pretty handsome yourself."

"You just gonna stand there and stare? Or are you gonna touch, too?"

When her tongue runs along her lower lip again, it takes everything in my power to stay rooted in place and let her close the distance between us.

"I think..." She pauses as her eyes roam over my chest. When they finally meet my eyes, she reaches for me. "I'd rather touch."

Chapter 15

Lanie

THE ENERGY SHIFTS in the room and I'm not sure who moves first. The moment our mouths meet again, Ryan devours me. I may have laid down the challenge, but he quickly takes control. His large hand rests at the nape of my neck and effectively changes the angle of our kiss by tugging lightly on my hair.

I seriously might combust on the spot.

As if he's reading my mind, "Fuck... you feel incredible," slips from his mouth between kisses from my jaw to my ear.

"Yes... right there..."

"I've been dying to taste you all day. You have no idea how difficult it's been to keep my hands to myself since lunch."

"Uh...why do you think... I went for a walk? I needed... a distraction," I say between kisses.

Hell, I can barely speak because my senses are on

overdrive as he explores my body. That's what this man does to me.

His laughter against my skin makes my inner muscles clench. I'm not sure if it's the combination of his touch, his words, or how hypersensitive I am, but I need more. When our bodies shift, the back of my legs meet the bed. On instinct, I tug him closer as I let myself fall onto the bed, taking him with me.

"Whoa." He laughs, bracing himself for the fall against the mattress. "You okay?"

Loving the weight of his body on mine, I grin triumphantly. "More than okay."

"Good," he says with a chaste kiss. "Let's get you further on this bed, so I can join you," he says, lifting me like a feather up the bed.

God. This man.

When he settles between my legs and leans forward on his elbows, I've never been more thankful for a queen-sized bed in my life. "Better?" he asks, brushing hair from my face.

"Absolutely." I grin in delight. Cupping my hand to his face, I pull him down for a kiss. God, I love the feel of his skin against mine and his scruff against my fingertips. I seriously can't get enough.

When he unclasps my bra and my breasts fall free, he pauses to take me in. His eyes heat as he licks his lips appreciating the view. His gaze sends shivers down my spine as my need for him grows.

With a lazy grin he caresses my skin. "God, you are so beautiful. You have no fucking clue what you do to me."

The moment his lips crash onto mine, all thoughts are lost. Electricity zings from my fingers to my toes as I cling to him, needing to feel his body against mine. He shifts down the bed, leaving a trail of hot wet kisses from my breasts to my belly button. Not being able to handle the sensory overload, my head falls back on the pillow and I just bask in the moment.

When he pauses, my focus returns to him to see what's wrong.

His hands rest at the button of my shorts and his eyes are waiting for mine.

"Mind if I take these off?"

Lifting my hips, I shove at the waist of my jean shorts and nod. "Please..."

Expertly, he slides himself and my clothes down until he's standing at the end of the bed. Never letting go of my gaze, his eyes roam over my body as he adjusts himself in his jeans.

God, that is the sexiest thing I've ever seen.

His eyes roam from the tip of my toes up to meet my eyes, and it takes everything in my power not to squirm in appreciation.

"Melanie, you are the sexiest fuckin' woman. I *love* your confidence and your curves."

Whoa. If that doesn't make my inner vixen stand up and take notice.

As if he doesn't have a care in the world, he slowly lifts one leg and plants a kiss near my inner ankle. It doesn't matter that I'm bare-assed naked, or that I'm basically dripping with need. No. Ryan takes his time to fulfill his promise and licks and kisses me everywhere.

By the time he reaches the top of my thighs I'm out of my freaking mind with need. Every nerve in my body is strung tight and I swear, he could simply blow his warm breath against me and I'll go off like a rocket.

The bastard takes his sweet fucking time kissing and caressing me everywhere, but where I need him most. He trails his sensual lips along my hips, up my ribs, and languishes over each breast.

"Ryan…" I moan in frustration.

And the asshole laughs. He fucking laughs.

"What, Melanie?"

"I need you…" I practically whine.

With a mischievous grin, he murmurs, "You've got me." While trailing his fingertips around the apex of my thighs.

Pointedly, I stare at his hand that's driving me wild and cock a brow in challenge.

He doesn't disappoint; he nudges my thighs further apart with his knee. Leaving me spread wide, he slowly drags his teasing fingertip up my thigh in slow circles and *finally* meets my request.

Dragging a finger from my core through my folds, he slowly circles my clit and repeats his efforts as he lazily asks, "Is this what you want?"

I open my mouth to say something, but my breath catches when he plunges a finger into me and grins knowingly.

We both watch as he slides his finger in and out of my soaking wet pussy.

"So fucking hot," he murmurs as he settles his head

between my legs. "Scooch up, so you can watch as I make you come with my mouth."

Yes, please. He doesn't have to tell me twice.

Slowly, he kisses up my thighs while his fingers play me like an instrument made just for him. When his warm breath blows across my soaking wet core, I tremble with need. "Ryan," I plead, fisting his hair.

I practically scream when his tongue slides along my lower lips to my clit. I'm so wound up, I could be speaking in tongues as I murmur my appreciation. This feels fucking insane. Without permission, my hips squirm as they move in rhythm with Ryan's expert hands.

As he continues to assault me with his wicked tongue, a firm arm rests against my abdomen to keep my hips in place. Once I'm where he wants me, he adds a second finger into the mix and I can't take it anymore.

I take matters into my own hands by gripping his hair and firmly guiding him to where I need it most.

I think he chuckles, but all I can hear is my pulse thundering in my ears. My senses are on overload as every muscle in my body gets tighter and tighter. The moment he pulls my clit between his lips and sucks hard, just as he flicks it with his tongue, I fucking come undone.

My rigidly stiff body thrashes as wave after wave of pure pleasure washes over me. Ryan's right there with me the entire way, pumping his fingers in and out, sucking and licking me through the most intense orgasm of my life.

When my body becomes too sensitive, he takes notice and slows his efforts, coaxing me through every twitch and pulse.

Eventually, his hand withdraws and he kisses his way up my body to rest beside me on the pillow.

Brushing the hair from my face, he whispers, "Hey there," as the sexiest smile spreads across his face. When his hand drops, he trails circles along my ribs and stomach as if he still feels the need to keep our contact.

"Hey yourself." I grin lazily when I realize that's about all the movement I can manage. "You may have broken me."

"In the best possible way, I hope."

I barely manage a nod. "Yep. Most definitely." My body feels like it is loaded down with lead weights and it takes every bit of effort I can muster to lift my hand to run along his muscular arm. "Just give me a minute and then it's my turn."

"That's not necessary."

Propping my head up with my hand, I turn to face him. "You can't rock a person's world and be like... no... I'm good... thanks. What gives?"

Gone is the confident man who ravaged my body mere minutes ago. He looks to the ceiling, and back at me before sighing heavily. "I want you... in every possible way, trust me," he groans before continuing. "But... I uh... was in a hurry this morning... and never even thought to bring condoms. I feel like a freaking dipshit."

I can't help it. I laugh at his forlorn expression. "You were a little preoccupied," I say, shifting my weight to sit up beside him.

"Wha... What are you doing, Lanie?" he asks as I straddle his waist with my naked body.

"Unfortunately, I don't have condoms either." Leaning forward, I kiss him.

When my sensitive breasts brush against his chest, my desire returns. As I sit up, I feel his straining dick through his pants, so I lean back and give it a gentle squeeze.

"Then wha.." I lean forward and cut him off with a kiss as I scooch down his body.

Quirking a brow, I throw down a challenge of my own. "I think it's your turn to lay back and watch for a while," I say, crawling off the end of the bed. When I reach his belt, I quickly undo it, along with the button of his jeans.

Leaning in to kiss his abdomen, I murmur, "Just remember, Ryan, two can play this game," I tease as I slide the tines of his zipper down.

Slowly I bring his jeans and boxer briefs with me.

I try not to get preoccupied when his cock springs free, but he notices when my tongue slides along my lip in appreciation.

"See something ya like?" he says as he strokes himself. It's long, thick, and pulsing at me. How can I not like it?

I slowly crawl up between his legs and pump it in my hand a few times before licking it from root to tip. "I guess you'll just have to find out," I rasp out before taking him in my mouth and showing him just how much I like what I see.

Chapter 16
Ryan

WHEN MY ALARM goes off the next morning, I have no doubt where I am. I know I'm in Lanie's bed and she's snuggled up next to me. Even though we couldn't have sex technically, we took turns wearing each other out, orally. Lanie's quite inventive and let's just say our shower is something I'll never forget.

Eventually, we got dressed and crawled into bed to actually sleep. Well—if dressed means a pair of sleep shorts and tank for her and boxer briefs for me. At least I had the forethought to bring an extra change of clothes so I don't have to rush around like a mad man to get back to work on time.

Why the hell I could remember pants, but not condoms is beyond me.

I guess it's because I didn't come over expecting to sleep with her—well, sexually. I didn't want to have a repeat of yesterday, so I threw in a change of clothes for today in case we conked out on the couch again.

Tracing imaginary circles along her spine, I let myself enjoy the moment. I've got at least a good hour until Jared shows up, and I'm not ready for my time with Lanie to end. These quiet moments with her are the best.

Don't get me wrong, I fuckin' loved exploring every inch of her body. But I've never met anyone like Melanie Lancaster. She's not only beautiful and sexy, but she's smart and thoughtful, too. Last night, I quickly found that our periods of time between our sexual exploration were just as enjoyable as rocking her world.

"What are you thinkin' about so hard over there?" comes in a raspy voice, which of course I find sexy as hell.

"Just thinkin' about you," I answer honestly.

"I'm not sure I can come again," she says, snuggling into my chest.

"I'm sure you will—eventually." I chuckle. "But that's not what I was thinking, Little Miss Horny Toad."

"Yeah, I'm the horny one."

"Whatever you say," I tease. "But to answer your question... I was just thinkin' about how much I've enjoyed my time with you—apart from orgasms—though those were mind-blowing."

On a yawn, she says, "I like spending time with you, too."

"Want to grab dinner tonight after your shift?"

I can hear her frown before I see it. "I can't. I'm closing."

"What about tomorrow night? Shit. Don't answer that. I forgot. Your sisters will be here."

"Wanna hang out at the festival with me on Saturday?"

Usually, I'd rather shave off my eyebrow before hanging out in town on one of the busiest weekends of the year, but if it means spending time with Lanie, I'll gladly make the sacrifice. "Yep. It's a date."

"Well, Mr. Murdock... you need to get ready for work. For some reason, I feel as if I could eat a horse this morning. Someone tired me out last night." Then her tone turns serious. "You get ready for work, and I'll make us breakfast." Quickly, she leans up to kiss me, then slides off her side of the bed, walks into the bathroom, and shuts the door.

A few minutes later, when she returns with a bright smile on her face, her hair is in a messy bun and she's grabbed a short cotton robe. Tying it at her waist, she cocks her head to the side. "You gonna get moving?"

"Just appreciating the view."

Rolling her eyes, she walks through the door before I can say another word.

It doesn't take me long to shower and change into my work clothes. As I pack my clothes back into my bag, I make a mental note to *never* go without condoms again. When I get downstairs, I put on my boots at the bar while she plates our omelets.

"Hope you don't mind mushroom and cheese. I didn't have time to fry bacon before Jared arrives."

"You're seriously spoiling me," I say, leaning in to kiss her cheek once she's beside me.

She shrugs as if this isn't a big deal and takes a bite. When she's done chewing, she adds, "I wasn't kidding when I said I'm starving. I didn't do this just for you."

After watching her yawn for the second time in a few minutes I ask, "Will you go back to bed once I leave?"

"Not likely. I doubt I'm tired enough to sleep through the banging outside."

Shit. Now I feel guilty for keeping her up all night. "I can give you the keys to my place and you can sleep over there."

Her face lights up with a beautiful smile. "As sweet as that offer is, I think I'll pass. I've got a few things to finish before the girls get here tomorrow. Besides, it's weird to invade your space without you there."

"Are you a coffee drinker?" I ask, thinking I could use a cup or three about now myself.

"Nope. Not really... wait, are you? I could've made you some."

"I only drink it when I'm desperate for caffeine. Usually, I'll grab an energy drink on campus if it's that bad."

"I might grab a chai latte today," she admits. "I can't do black coffee. I require too much cream and sugar for it to still be considered coffee. If I'm out, want me to bring you something back?"

"No need. But thanks."

Glancing at the clock, I shovel the last bite of my breakfast into my mouth and stand to clear my plate. Seeing that she's done, I swipe hers, too, then quickly rinse them off and put them in the dishwasher. Grabbing the pan from the stove, I make quick work of washing it as well, then wipe down the counters, so Lanie doesn't have to.

When I turn around I catch her watching my every move.

"See something ya like?" I tease as memories from last night flood my mind.

"I've got one word for you, Murdock," she says with a heavy sigh.

"Really? What's that?" I ask, playing along.

"Condoms."

This isn't where I thought she was going with this.

"Condoms?"

"Yep... Let's not forget them in the future."

Chapter 17
Lanie

BY THE TIME my sisters arrive Friday evening, I am wound up with excitement. It's only been about a month since I drove up to Gonzaga to see them, but it feels like forever.

The moment they walk through the door, I am up off the couch squeezing the life out of them.

"God I've missed you two. I've ordered pizza and picked up gelato from your favorite store downtown."

"Thank god," Raven moans. "Sloane wouldn't let us stop to get anything to eat because she knew you'd do something like this."

"Hey," Sloane cries out in defense. "You were also the one complaining how you needed to get here so you can work early in the morning."

Rolling her eyes, Raven walks to the kitchen. "You know I have to start work early tomorrow with the festival this weekend. I would've left last night if this trip was up to me."

"Well, you're here now," I remind them. "Let's grab your things from the car and eat. I'm starving."

By the time we unload their car and eat dinner, the sun is setting, so I suggest we go sit on the back deck to watch it like we used to when we were kids.

Settling onto the Adirondack chairs we have on the back deck, Sloane yawns. "I for one am looking forward to sleeping in tomorrow."

"I wish," Raven groans. "I start first thing in the morning—with the festival starting tomorrow."

"What are your plans, Lanie?" Sloane asks, stifling another yawn.

Laughing at how pathetic she looks trying to pretend she's not exhausted, I suggest, "You should go to bed, Sloane. You're beat."

Her voice fills with genuine concern. "You won't mind?"

"We've got all summer. Go—get some sleep."

Sloane stands and gives each of us a hug. "Sorry, I was up last night cramming for my final this morning. I'll see you in the morning. Love you."

When it's just Raven and me, I take the time to check in with her. "Are you sure you want to work at the ropes course tomorrow?"

"Yeah. The money's great and I want to help out." Then she looks me up and down with care. "Have you been okay being here alone?"

"Yeah, I really have," I assure her. "I think the most difficult time was when I first arrived. But being here—even without Nana, always brings me peace, ya know?"

"I swear, the house still smells like her," Raven muses.

"Well, that's because she still had a shitload of air fresheners," I pointedly remind her. "She bought so many; I swear we'll still be using it when we have kids of our own."

Raven's quiet for a long moment as she stares into the purple, orange, and yellow sunset. It's nearly dark and there's just a sliver of light left. Between the constant whir of the wind and the beautiful horizon, we sit in silence until the sky turns a dark navy blue against the horizon.

It's Raven who breaks the silence with a whisper, "I miss her."

"So do I, Raven. So do I."

*****

I'm cleaning up the kitchen the next morning when there's a knock at the door. Sloane's upstairs sleeping and Raven just left for work. Hoping our unexpected visitor won't ring the doorbell, I rush to the door.

To my surprise, Ryan's on the other side with a cup of coffee in one hand and a bouquet of wildflowers in the other. "Hey, I wasn't expecting you for another hour or so."

"Hope you don't mind. I was in the area and couldn't wait that long to see you."

Oh, my heart. Could he be any sweeter?

When I hesitate, he misunderstands and quickly says, "Would you rather I come back later?"

"No... not at all. Come in." Stepping to the side, I make room for him to enter.

"Here, these are for you," he says, handing me both the

flowers and cup in his hand. "It's an Oregon Chai. That's what you said you liked yesterday, right?"

My chest tightens as butterflies swarm in my belly at the gesture. "Yeah. You got it right. But you didn't have to get me one."

"Well, I know you stayed up late last night visiting with your sisters and I wanted to do something nice for you."

Looking around the house he asks, "Where are they?"

"Raven's at work and Sloane's sleeping," I reply as I find a vase for the flowers. "I'm fairly certain she'll sleep until noon. We were up pretty late last night."

"Why were you up so early then?" he asks, standing at the counter beside me. "You've got me trained to be up before eight," I tease. We have been texting for the past hour, so he shouldn't be surprised I'm awake.

"Har... Har..." Changing the subject, he asks, "Have you eaten?"

"I've had some grapes; does that count?"

Ryan's dopey grin makes me laugh. "It's about time I get to treat you to a meal. Grab your things and let's get going before tourists fill up the town."

Seeing as it's nearly nine, I highly doubt that.

"First, let me grab my books I want signed by the authors today."

Rushing upstairs, I quickly brush my teeth and comb through my hair. Then I grab my tote bag and purse and join Ryan in the kitchen who greets me with a panty-melting smile.

When he sees my bag, he eyes it quizzically. "Isn't the point of going to a signing—to get books there?"

"Oh, I'll get more. Trust me. Since many authors are traveling from out of state to attend, their supply is limited. They've encouraged us to bring our own books if we want them signed."

Ryan links his hand in mine as he drives us across town to his favorite diner. When we find lines stacked along the sidewalks, he suggests grabbing something in Manzanita, a few towns south of Seaside. Usually, tourists who come for the festival stay close to Seaside or Cannon Beach, and if we go just a little further, we might find a diner that's not packed with people.

After placing our orders at the small hole-in-the wall diner we found about twenty minutes away, Ryan reaches for my hand. "I know you're busy for the next two weekends with your family, but what are your plans for the weekend after?"

"Most likely work, but I don't have my schedule yet, why?"

Taking a sip of his orange juice, he casually states, "I'm going back to CRU for the weekend for a wedding. I'd love for you to be my date."

"Won't the bride go crazy having last minute guests?" Surely, he knows this, right?

Ryan shakes his head adamantly. "Not at all... In fact, it's mainly just family and friends. It's taking place in their backyard and there's no formal head count—besides, I'm allowed a plus one."

"Oh, Ryan," I say, shaking my head at his logic. "There's always a head count at weddings. Trust me. Even if it's just a small wedding, I'll stick out like a sore thumb."

"Look, Vince is my best friend. It's his sister getting

married… and well… they don't have many people in their corner besides the friends they've made since college—but that's their story to tell. There's nothing I won't do for either of them. I'm not sure how many people are coming from the groom's side of the family, but from my understanding, it will only be his siblings and grandparents, along with their closest friends."

"Are you sure?" Taking a date to a wedding is a big deal—at least I consider it a big deal for such an important event.

When he pins me with those beautiful blue eyes, my heart skips a beat. "Look—total disclosure. I'm selfish. I know you're busy for the next few weeks and I really like spending time with you. I still have my apartment near campus so it won't cost us a ton of money. And… I promise… I'll bring more condoms than we can possibly need."

"Ohmigod." I gasp, coving my mouth as I look around to see if anyone's heard this sudden declaration. Then I hiss in disbelief, "You did *not* just say that."

Instead of answering, he deflects, "You're the one who made me promise to *never* forget them."

"Touché." He's got me there.

The moment he knows he's won, a triumphant smile spreads over his face. "And before you attempt any more excuses, it's a summertime, backyard wedding. No one other than the bride and the groom are even wearing formal attire. I'm wearing a pair of slacks and a button-up and any summer dress you own will be perfect."

"You say they're from school. Will I know anyone?"

Letting out a heavy breath, he shrugs. "It depends."

"On..." I prompt, wondering why he seems hesitant.

"Whether you follow sports, I guess."

Crossing my arms over my chest, I demand, "Explain."

"Well, I'm pretty sure a few guys from the basketball team will be there. Drew is pretty tight with Vince's girlfriend, Sydney. His roommates, Grey and DeShawn, have been hanging out there a lot this spring... well, ever since Vanessa found out Grey couldn't cook to save his life."

"Okay..." I draw out, mulling over the names. I know of them, but don't know any of the players personally. "Anyone else I might know?"

"Well, Damien—the groom, his sister is Charlotte Anne— the author you're seeing today. I'm sure she and her husband, Luke, will be there."

My jaw drops to the floor in the way that he mentions this so casually.

He continues before I can process his words. "I haven't officially met either of them, but I'm sure it's just a matter of time. Don't say anything about it today when you meet. She already lives in a fishbowl with her husband being the head coach for the Rainier Renegades. I don't want to take away her anonymity."

"I... I don't even know what to say," I ponder in awe over the information he's dumped on me.

He shrugs as if my decision should be simple. "Say yes. Say you'll go and be my date to the wedding. I need to at least make an appearance and help out where I can."

"When are you leaving?" I ask, wondering if I can make this happen.

"I'm heading to CRU Thursday afternoon for the bachelor party, but the wedding's Saturday."

"I'm not sure I can take that much time off." When his shoulders slouch and his face fills with disappointment, I quickly add, "But I'll ask for Saturday and Sunday off. Worse case, I'll drive myself back to campus. It's not like I haven't done it a million times before."

Reaching across the table, Ryan squeezes my hand. "Thanks, Lanie."

Chapter 18
Ryan

"I WAS NOT PREPARED FOR THIS," I mutter more to myself than to Lanie, who's a few steps ahead of me. We've been at the book signing for less than five minutes and I've already been practically run over by a wagon of books.

A wagon. I can't make this shit up.

This woman in her mid-fifties had it stacked to the point of overflowing, took a corner too quickly, and nearly took me out in the process. She was on a mission to see Stone Ryder and I was clearly in her way.

I've quickly learned, these book women mean business when they step into this event. Some have spreadsheets of books they've preordered and purchased. Others have the map marked for where their favorite authors are. All are zipping around with great purpose and are ready to fangirl at the drop of a hat.

Lanie's approach is far more casual as she leads me from

table to table checking out books to be read. At first, we were holding hands, but now that she's picked up a few more paperbacks, I've volunteered to be her Sherpa. She signed up for a VIP bag, so now she has two large totes. Of course, being the gentleman I am, I volunteered to carry them. They're not too heavy—yet. But they have enough room in them for the potential.

When we get to Charlotte's table I recognize her husband, Luke Leighton, standing beside her. I'm a huge fan of the Rainier Renegades and I've followed his career since he was drafted. Taking Lanie's lead, I wait in line beside her.

Right before it's her turn to get her books signed, she turns to me. "Can I see the blue bag? I've got a few of her books in there. I'm also getting her latest two because I only have the e-books."

"Sounds good. Just let me know what you need help with."

"Ahhh..." Luke drawls out in his Tennessee accent to Lanie, "I see you've already got him trained good and proper for events like these." To me, he conspiratorially whispers, "Just carry the bags—and agree to everything she wants to buy."

"Now that's my kinda guy," Charlotte muses as she pats her husband's arm. "Did ya see his shirt, Luke?"

"That's where Dame works, right?"

Before she can answer for him, I nod in agreement. "Yeah. He's actually a friend of mine... well, a friend of a friend... as his fiancée's brother, Vince, is my best friend."

Both Charlotte and Luke's eyes widen in surprise, but it's Luke that says, "Then you must know Jules."

Chuckling, I nod. "Yeah. She's got us all wrapped around her finger—especially her unks'. I've been friends with the Larsons since freshman year."

Charlotte holds a hand to her chest and grins. "I still can't believe Dame's getting married. Though he couldn't have picked a better person as a partner—and that Jules—well, she's just as precious as they come."

"Yes, she is," I agree. "I'm Ryan by the way, and this is Lanie. It's a pleasure to meet you both."

Luke turns his attention to Lanie, who's holding up three books for Charlotte to sign. "Nice to meet you, Lanie. Can I take those so Charlotte can get them signed for you?"

"I'd also like both books from the *Finding Our Way* duet." Luke picks up the books she mentions and hands them to Charlotte to sign.

"Do you want these made out to you?" Charlotte asks, pen at the ready.

Lanie smiles eagerly. "Just Lanie is fine." Then she spells it out for Charlotte to write a quick note and then signs her name.

When Luke states how much the books will cost, I hand over the cash before Lanie can reach for her purse. This causes both Charlotte and Luke to laugh. But it's Luke who says, "That boy's a keeper, Darlin'. He not only schleps the books, but he'll buy ya more."

"Before you go, can I get a picture for my readers' group?" Charlotte asks, stepping next to her sign. Luke takes a few shots and I grab some as well so I can share them with Lanie.

Eventually, Lanie's books are stowed in the tote bag and we say our goodbyes. Then we move on to the next table.

By the time we get through Stone Ryder's line, Lanie and I are both ready to call it a day. I have mad respect for those who come prepared with lists and their wagons. I will never doubt the use of wagons again—lesson learned.

By the time we walk from the book signing to Lanie's, we're exhausted. We plop onto the couch and I pull her into my side so we can snuggle for a while. As much as I'd love to spend the entire day with her, I'm expected in about an hour at my parents' place to help my dad move some equipment.

When Lanie's not her usual talkative self, I look down to see her eyes drifting closed. "Hey," I whisper and her eyes dart open. "If I stay here, we'll both fall asleep. I'm gonna go. I'll text you when I'm done helping my dad."

"Okay," she says with a yawn, and I'm not entirely sure she's heard me.

The moment I extricate myself from her, she stretches out across the entire couch. I take the blanket that she's struggling to fix from her and cover her. Then I bend down to kiss her on the forehead as I whisper, "Get some sleep."

Chapter 19
Lanie

AS MUCH AS I love my sisters, I selfishly miss my time with Ryan. Sure, I've seen him these last few days while he worked on the house. We've stolen a few kisses now and then, but we haven't spent any quality time together since Saturday. It's weird, but I actually miss him. Talking on the phone and texting just isn't the same.

Raven, Sloane, and I have a rare afternoon off and we've agreed to spend it together. We're grabbing a pizza and watching chick-flicks all night. As the twins watch the movie, my focus has been on Ryan as he works on the side of the house. When a pillow flies into my lap, I look at Raven and ask, "What the heck was that for?"

Raven looks at Sloane then back at me. "I don't know. Why do you think I threw the pillow at her?"

"Uh, maybe because you called her name three times and she completely ignored you?"

Raven and Sloane are identical twins, but they are complete opposites when you look at them now. Raven's dressed in black leggings and an oversized sweatshirt, whereas Sloane looks like she just stepped off a runway—in full makeup and dressed in her black pencil skirt and white blouse from work.

They're both absolutely gorgeous. But at the moment they're both staring daggers at me and it's obvious I'm about to be ganged up on. Their matching hazel eyes are laser focused on me, and if I'm not careful, shit will go sideways in a nanosecond.

Knowing they'd see right through a complete lie, I go with a half-truth as I shrug it off, "I guess I was just zoning out."

"And this doesn't have anything to do with the hot builder outside?"

Just then Jared walks by and again I deflect. "Uh… that guy's practically old enough to be our dad. There's no way I'm interested in him."

At least that part is true.

"Yeah." Sloane rolls her eyes at Raven and I swear they're doing their freaky twin communication. "That's not who we're talking about…"

"Neither of you know what you're talking about," I grumble. "Go back to watching the show."

I probably should know what we're watching, but that would mean my focus is off Ryan—so it doesn't happen. As the girls silently exchange more thoughts with one another, I force myself to pay attention to the television. Of course, Ryan chooses this exact time to walk by the window and I might as well be that dog in the movie *UP*, completely distracted by squirrels.

When the movie ends, the twins head upstairs to finish unpacking, so I use this opportunity to temporarily flee. "I'm gonna check the mail!" I holler up the stairs, then dart outside, hoping I haven't missed him. Thankfully, Ryan's still sitting in his truck, talking on his phone—like he does most nights.

When he spots me approaching, he ditches his phone and steps outside to greet me. With each of their rooms facing the sides of the house, I feel fairly confident approaching Ryan and letting him wrap me into a hug.

"I've missed you," he says when he releases me.

"Same," I agree on a sigh.

"I know you're hanging with your sisters tonight, but how about dinner at my place tomorrow after work?"

The thought of uninterrupted time with Ryan sounds magnificent.

Then, I remember why I can't and I feel as if I've just been given a lead balloon.

Groaning, I quickly explain, "As soon as I get off, we're driving to Dad's in Tacoma. Lizzy's graduation is Thursday, and my mom flew into town so we won't be back until Friday evening."

"Do you have a few minutes right now? You keep lookin' over your shoulder as if you expect someone to be watching you."

That's because they probably are. I internally groan.

We walk along the house and across the paved path of the promenade. As if he senses my need for privacy once we're out of sight of the house he reaches for my hand and pulls me closer to him and loops an arm around my waist. "Everything okay?"

Being in his arms feels better than I would've imagined. I'm not sure how someone I barely know can have this sort of impact on me. But it just feels... right.

When I don't say anything, he stops and turns to face me. "What's going on in that head of yours?"

Sheepishly, I shrug. "Would you believe, I just got lost in the moment with you holding me?"

"Ha... you have no idea," he says before leaning down and pressing his lips to mine.

This isn't a kiss that gets carried away, or full of all-consuming passion. No, it's light and tender with a promise of more.

When he breaks our kiss, he leans his forehead against mine and asks with a grin, "We good?"

"Better than good," I whisper, running my thumb along his jaw.

As he turns to continue our walk he asks, "How are things with your sisters today?"

"They got in late. It's nice to finally have them here. I miss them so much."

"I imagine that's hard for you."

"Yeah, it will be weird having us all here for the summer without Nana. I'm sure we'll be fine—but she was the glue that held my sisters and I together when World War III would threaten to rage. I love my sisters fiercely, but it doesn't mean we always like each other."

"I'm fairly certain all families are like that. Though I'm sure now that you're older, it will be easier to manage."

"That's just it—I'm the oldest. With my parents divorced, I'm now the one everyone turns to for support. Usually, I know what to do, but sometimes... well... let's just say, I make it up as I go."

Ryan's deep laugh sends shivers up my spine. "Lanie, I hate to break it to you, but I'm fairly certain if you would've asked your grandma—or any adult for that matter, that's what they're all doing."

"But I just feel so... lost... sometimes," I admit, not knowing where this sudden vulnerability comes from.

"I haven't met your sisters, but I'm sure if you explained this to them, they'd probably be strong enough to let you lean on them, too."

He's right. I know.

"And for the record, if you let me... I can be here for you, too."

Chapter 20

Lanie

IT'S BEEN A LONG WEEK. Between my sister's graduation, spending time with my parents, and doing all things together as a family, I'm exhausted. We got back into town late last night and with the party today, I've got a lot going on.

To my surprise, when I step out onto the deck and look around, the siding on this side has been completed. Even though they still need to finish one last side, not one single thing from this vantage point would let anyone know construction was happening on our property.

Dad had paid a lawn care service to come out a few times a month to maintain the property and to keep the appearance that people were still around. It had been his gift to Nana when she was alive, and it was a gift to us girls now that she's gone. But the lawn care service only maintains the yard. They don't plant new things. Since my sisters are still sleeping and Dad is, by all standards, a brown thumb, I can't help but smile when I see the flower boxes that had once only been growing dirt are now filled with purple and blue flowers in full bloom.

As I look further, I notice the shrubs that had been overgrown are now pruned back. Wait, is it possible the cement pathway leading to the promenade is now brighter?

Pulling out my phone I take a picture of the scene before me and shoot off a text.

Me: Did you have anything to do with this?

Immediately there's a reply and my stomach flips in anticipation.

Ryan: Maybe… are you okay with it?

No longer wanting to bother with texting, I immediately dial and he picks up on the first ring with a laugh. "Well, good morning to you, too."

"You seriously came over on your day off and helped clean up the place?"

"Again… are you okay with it?"

"Yes, but that's not the point," I huff.

Immediately, he counters. "Well, what is your point?"

Trying to find words for my overwhelming emotions, I sputter, "You…. didn't… you… shouldn't…"

I can hear the smile in his voice when he prompts, "I didn't ask or I shouldn't care?"

"You… didn't have to do any of it," I finally spit out.

"I know I didn't," he pointedly reminds me. "But I thought it would make your day easier. Speaking of which, is there anything I can do to help you this afternoon?"

Shaking my head in disbelief of his incredible kindness, I just stare out at the ocean.

"Lanie? Can I help you with anything else?"

Remembering I need to use my words, I mutter, "No... but if you're not busy, you're welcome to stop by. Dad hired caterers and there will be plenty of food to eat."

"Does your family even know about me?" He laughs.

"They know who you are," I grumble, avoiding the question he's really asking.

"Okay, then..." he draws out. "I'm supposed to help Jared with a project he's doing at his house for a bit this afternoon, but if I get done early enough, I'll try and stop by."

The thought of seeing him brings a smile to my face. "Okay. Sounds good."

Lizzy suddenly appears on the back deck, interrupting our conversation. "There you are." Looking around the yard her mouth drops. "Wow. The place looks good. Did you do all this?"

"Uh..." How do I explain? "No. Ryan did."

Puzzled, she asks, "Who's Ryan?"

From the other end of the phone I hear Ryan chuckle. "And that's my cue. I'll see ya later, Lanie."

Before I can utter a word, he hangs up.

"Ryan?" Who is Ryan? He's our contractor, but that's not what she's asking, is it?

I've always kept my private life as much as I could—private. It just made it easier and less hassle. In case things didn't work out, it just made sense not to let my younger siblings get attached.

Raven comes through the door before I can respond with a smirk. "Ryan?"

Lizzy looks from me to Raven and says, "Yeah, I was just asking who he is."

Dad chooses this moment to arrive and naively says, "Ryan's the contractor Mom hired, right? Well, the contractor's son."

Yeah. I'm not explaining who Ryan really is with Dad here. Ryan and I haven't even discussed anything about what we are in terms of a relationship. I'm not about to tell my siblings, in front of my dad, how I really feel about him.

"Yes... He's the one Nana hired to help with the house." Again—I'm not lying.

Lizzy eyes me suspiciously, but with Dad here, I know neither her nor Raven will press the issue.

We love our dad; he will be in your corner one thousand percent. But he is not the one we *ever* went to for relationship advice. He's well... militant. He doesn't deal with things like getting emotional about boy troubles. Besides, he's way too intimidating to willingly subject anyone to who *might* only be potential boyfriend material. If you're not certain that's the guy you want to be with, it's best not to bring him around.

"I just got a call from my buddy, Enzo. He's bringing his family down for the day to celebrate Lizzy's graduation. You all remember him, right? He's got twin boys about... gosh, I think four, and his oldest is actually attending CRU—you might know her. Her name is Maddie—shoot, I don't know her last name because it's actually his stepdaughter. I served with him in Germany before he retired."

Raven glances to Lizzy and it's obvious they're clueless as to who he's talking about. But I think I remember meeting them when Dad came home for Enzo's wedding a few years ago. But I wouldn't know them if they passed me on the street.

"Anyway... Let me know when they arrive." Then he turns to my sister. "Raven, will you and Sloane help me set up the decorations she insisted we buy? I've got a bit of time and I want everything to run smooth for Lizzy's big day."

"I'm on my way to pick up the cake from the bakery," I say as we all disperse to get things ready for the party.

OVERALL, I'd say the graduation party was a success. Dad played the role of proud parent since Mom's client needed her back in California. My sisters hung out with their friends and I got to visit with family and friends I haven't seen in years.

Eventually, it split up into two places. While Dad and his friends stayed near the house, Lizzy and her friends took it upon themselves to create a fire and make s'mores on the beach. I just restocked the chocolate and marshmallows when Lizzy finally makes an appearance away from the adults.

"I see you finally escaped," I tease, pulling her into a hug.

"I love our family and friends, but if I get asked *what's next*, one more time, I might just throat punch someone."

"It's the obligatory question of the day. When you get older, it will be... so... *when are you gonna settle down?*"

This causes my sister to double over in laughter. "But

speaking of settling down… what's up with you and that Ryan guy?"

"Nothing to tell…" I quickly dismiss.

"Hmmm…" she draws out as a group of locals my age approach the fire to hang out with us.

"Hmmm, what?" I probe.

"Raven and Sloane seem to think there's something going on between you."

"And you believe them?"

She suddenly growls, "Gahh… when are you gonna stop treating me with kid gloves, Lanie? I've watched your face light up all weekend when you'd receive a text and thought I wouldn't notice. I'm not an idiot. You like someone… is it this Ryan guy or someone else?"

"What makes you so sure it's a guy?"

Raising her voice as her frustration with me grows. she shrugs. "Hell, if it's a girl, I'm happy for you. Because the point is… I… want… you… happy."

"Well, thank you," I huff in exasperation. "But for the record… I'm into guys."

"Any guys? Or one in particular?" My sister raises a brow in challenge.

"I don't see that's any of your business."

"Okay… I didn't think it would come to this, but I'm pulling out my summer dare."

Shit. As a kid, we made a pact.

We each decided we would either tell the truth, no exceptions—or accept the dare—no matter the stakes if we weren't ready to divulge the information demanded. Part of the pact is that we only get to use it on each other once each summer so we needed to make it count.

Squaring my shoulders, I put on my poker face. The one that's well perfected that I learned from Nana when I want the girls to see I show no fear. Nodding once in her direction, I agree, "Okay, what are the stakes?"

Licking her lower lip, she looks into the fire for a few moments. Thankfully, there's no one within earshot of whatever it is she's about to lay down.

Giving me an out, she asks, "You sure you just don't wanna tell me what's going on with Ryan?"

I can't tell you—because I don't know myself, is what I want to yell, but instead, I repeat my words, showing no weakness. "What are the stakes?"

"You're either gonna tell me what's going on with Ryan..." she draws out for effect. "Or you're gonna walk up and kiss the next single guy our age that walks up to the fire."

Is she freaking kidding me? At least she made the stipulation of being single and our age—or that would be gross.

As if the pressure wasn't already on, I spot movement coming down the path, though I can't tell who it is.

"You gonna tell me, or do I need to loan you my Chapstick?" the monster beside me taunts. My little sprout has grown into a fine manipulator. She knows how to run a fine bargain. And she knows I won't kiss a total stranger.

But what the fuck am I gonna do?

The moment the person walking up the path reveals himself; my body knows the answer before words can kick in.

I stomp right up and within seconds I'm reaching for his face, pulling his lips onto mine.

Chapter 21
Ryan

THE MOMENT I make it out of the path and onto the beach, I see her stomping in my direction. She doesn't smile or greet me the way she usually does. In fact, she almost looks pissed.

What the hell did I do?

Without stopping—like a normal person would, in one fluid movement she marches right into my personal space, lifts up on her toes, and reaches for my face. Her eyes are heated and her voice coarse as she demands, "Kiss me."

Yeah, I don't need to be told twice.

Much to my dismay, we've been sneaking around her sisters all week. She'd been afraid of her sisters getting the wrong impression.

Apparently, she no longer has any fucks to give.

I'm not sure what's changed, but you won't hear any complaints from me.

Her tongue sweeps against my lips and I part them to

invite her in. Her kiss is greedy and filled with need. It's sexy as hell to see this dominant side of her. I love a woman who takes exactly what she needs.

Hell... I love this woman... period.

Whoa... where did that thought come from?

She may have started this kiss, but the moment my body realizes what my brain just revealed, I quickly take control—and I don't hold back.

I kiss her like a man in love—because I love this woman.

Lifting her off the ground, I stand to my full height. With her in my arms, I feel as if I can accomplish anything. I no longer want to sit back and wait for life to happen. I want it to begin fight fuckin' now—and I don't care who's around to see.

When the beach fills with cat calls and a loud, "Get a room," I realize maybe I do care—and this isn't the best place to have my sudden epiphany about Lanie.

Slowly I let her body slide against mine as I set her back on the sand while the crowd goes wild with hoots, hollers, applause, and even some whistles.

Lanie's face is tomato red and I'm fairly certain my cheeks are, too, if the burning I feel is any indication.

Running a hand over her mouth, she impishly shrugs. "Sorry. Got carried away."

"That was...." I peer at the crowd loosely formed around us, "one of the fucking hottest kisses I've ever experienced. Don't you dare apologize," comes out fierce and demanding.

"In fact, if you ever feel the need to do it again, I'm the only one you'd better be kissing like that. M'kay?"

Her lips quirk as her tongue runs slowly along her teeth.

"I've got an idea." She purses her lips and I can see her wheels turning.

"Does it involve more kisses like that?"

"Yeah, but first. Let's go officially introduce you to my sister, Lizzy. Then what do you say we get out of here and finish what we started?"

Leaning in so only she can hear I whisper, "I've stocked up on condoms."

BEFORE LANIE CAN RESPOND, a girl I recognize from pictures around the house approaches.

"So... you must be Ryan..." Lizzy holds out a hand to shake. "This one..." she points to her sister, "won't tell me a thing about you, but that ovary popping kiss she just laid on you spoke volumes. Hell, I think I could get pregnant from just watching the two of you from afar."

"That's not how it works." Lanie laughs at her sister.

"It will for you if you're not careful."

Damn, her sister's a spitfire. I like it.

"Well, on that note...I guess you're officially no longer a baby, so I don't need to shield you anymore." Lanie tugs at my arm. "We're gonna go be *very careful*—and prove your theory wrong."

Did she really just tell her sister and anyone who is listening we're leaving to have sex?

The next thing I know, we're walking down the path back to her house.

Once we're out of sight from everyone, she stops and

doubles over with laughter. "That little shit."

"What are you talking about?"

"My sister's as manipulative as they come. She knew I had feelings for you, but I wouldn't admit it. So, she laid down a summer dare—and damn... she got me good."

"Summer dare?" I ask, completely confused.

"Extremely long story short, I either have to tell the truth or take the dare... it's how I've always gotten my sisters to spill the beans when I wanted to learn something about them... but damn, the student has become the teacher."

"And this dare was..." I draw out, hoping she'll fill in the dots to her cryptic thoughts.

Eventually, she admits, "To kiss the next guy who walked up to the party." Then she tilts her head to the side and asks, "Wait... how did you know I was here?"

"Uh, your sister Raven told me."

"Oh, that brat, I'd bet anything they were both in on it."

"Wait... was that all done on a dare?" I ask, feeling very defensive at the moment.

Pointing to the beach, she laughs again. "That was *exactly* how it was supposed to be. You have no idea how much I've missed you this week. Now we don't have to sneak around because apparently, I wasn't fooling anyone."

Feeling a little on edge, I ask, "Am I just a pawn in this game of yours?"

"Oh, god, no." She stops and looks me dead in the eye. "I was. I really like you, Ryan. It just took a push from her to admit it."

Relief washes through me and she notices.

"Shit. I really fucked this up, didn't I?"

Fuck. She'll never understand my reaction unless I start from the beginning.

Taking her hand, I lead her on a path parallel between the house and the beach, away from anyone we know. "Let's go for a walk and I'll explain."

We walk in silence until we can no longer hear any of the partygoers. When we get to a large log, I sit down and pat the spot next to me, hoping she'll do the same.

She worries her lip as she massages her hands. Wanting to put her out of her misery, I take her hand and link my fingers through hers and I lay out my truth.

"First. You haven't fucked anything up, or at least not as far as I'm concerned. But there're some things that are non-negotiable with me, and I need you to be aware of them, so we can hold each other accountable."

"Okay," she draws out and waits, slightly calmer than before for me to continue.

"You see, I don't have a lot of experience with dating. I was that quiet, shy guy who was always the friend, but never the boyfriend. If I crushed on someone, I did it from afar. I was the friend they could count on, and I didn't want to add any pressure to them because they were going through a lot and the timing was never right."

"Okay...." she draws out again, but I can see questions turning in her head.

"But over this last year, I've decided I'm no longer gonna be that guy on the sidelines. If I like someone, I'm gonna tell them. If they feel the same, great. If they don't, then I'll move on."

"I guess…" She starts staring at the sunset, then turns to face me. "I don't understand what this has to do with us?"

"Freshman year, I met this girl…"

"So this is really about someone specific." Christ, she's already drawing her own conclusions, so I'd better just spit it out.

"Yeah. I guess it is…"

"Did she hurt you?"

"Not in the way you think… she was actually innocent in it all, but that doesn't mean I wasn't hurt in the process.

"You see, I met this girl freshman year. She was going through a rough time, so I started out being just a friend she could count on. But as the years went on, she essentially became the girl I compared all others to. She'd been through a lot and wasn't ready to date, so I just sat back and waited."

"What changed?"

Shrugging, I rip the Band-Aid off, "She met someone who got her attention and I watched her fall deliriously happy in love."

"Wow, that had to hurt."

Leave it to Lanie to empathize with me.

"Yeah. It wasn't the easiest thing—that's for sure."

"The point I'm trying to make is that if you have feelings for me—tell me. Don't make me wait and wonder. I'm not making the mistake of sitting on the sidelines ever again. I like you. I wanna be with you. I don't want you to have to be tricked into telling me how you feel. Please shoot from the hip and give it to me straight. That's all I ask."

"I do like you, Ryan. I'm just used to being the oldest sister—who's kept her business to herself when it comes to guys. You'll soon find out when you meet my dad, he's a straight shooter, too, as you say. If you come sniffing around and you're not sure about staying—he's been known to run guys off. It's been engrained since I was old enough to know better, to keep my private life private until I knew they were in it for the long haul."

"I get it," I offer when she finally takes a breath.

Then another thought hits me.

"Just how many guys were in it for the long haul?"

"That's what you pick out of that ramble?"

"Well, are we talking a handful or dozens?"

Her eyes bug out as she laughs. "Dozens? Yeah—No. I'd say three made the cut. Two were in high school—so those don't count—we were young and innocent. Only one since college."

"And were there many that didn't make the cut with your dad?"

Blowing out a long breath, she shrugs. "I'm not overtly promiscuous—but as you well know, I'm not a virgin either. But to answer your question there's a few that Dad doesn't know about."

Turning the table, she asks, "Where do you fall? You said you had a crush on this girl for years, so were you holding out for her? Or were you just keeping her as a place holder on your heart while you fooled around with other women?"

Okay. She's definitely shooting straight—but I asked for this.

"For the longest time, she *was* it for me. Sure, I dated others and some led to sex and I, too, am not a virgin, but I wasn't a man whore or anything.

"So where does all this leave us?"

"Well, I like you. You like me. I'm... not ready for a family." She shivers. "Sorry, that brought flashbacks of Barney, but I am open to the possibility, and if what you say is true, I'd like that possibility to be with you to see where things go."

Chuckling at where her brilliant mind went, I agree with her. "I'd like that, too."

"And... there's something I'd like you to do tonight before you go home."

"Anything..." I say without hesitation.

"I think it's time for you to meet my family—as my boyfriend."

As I process the meaning behind her words, I grin. "I most certainly think that can be arranged—on one condition..."

"What's that?"

"You come home with me to meet mine."

Chapter 22
Lanie

USUALLY WHEN I'M on long drives, I listen to music or an audio book. Today, I'm contemplating the events of this past week. When Ryan and I walked back to the house, all three of my sisters looked as if they were the cats that ate the canary. They knew exactly what they were doing... and if I wasn't supposed to be mad at them for tricking me, I probably would've hugged the shit out of them, because since that night I've never been happier.

I think the key to Dad meeting future boyfriends for my sisters is to do it when he's hanging out with his friends. Maybe those few beers he'd been drinking helped, too. Or perhaps, Dad knew without a doubt Ryan is someone I'm interested in, and so for now, he's giving Ryan a shot.

Either way, it was a rather anticlimactic introduction. They shook hands, drank a beer together, and Dad essentially welcomed him with open arms. I'd almost say Dad was losing his touch until Raven brought over the guy she'd met at work this last week. Then the dad I knew was back with a vengeance. I felt sorry for Kirk. I think he may have pissed himself before scurrying home with his tail between his legs. Raven wasn't impressed so I doubt they'll see each other again.

As I pull into Ryan's apartment complex, I'm surprised to find he lives across the street from me. Literally, I can actually see my kitchen window from his doorstep. Talk about a small world. We'd been less than a hundred yards from each other and we had to go to Seaside to meet. Go figure.

I don't even get to knock before his door swings open. I've got an overnight bag slung over my shoulder with my purse, and my dress on a hanger in my hand.

"Here, let me take that," Ryan offers, leading me into his apartment. "It's only a one-bedroom, but it's mine."

"You're lucky. I'm getting a new roommate next year and I'm a little nervous."

Setting my bag on his bed, he takes my dress and hangs it on a hook behind his bedroom door. "I'm sure it'll be fine," he says as he turns and reaches for me.

"Mmmm... I've missed you," I moan as I breathe in his delicious scent.

"It's been a long three days," he says, pulling me closer. "I couldn't wait for you to get here."

Tipping up on my toes, I press my lips to his and whisper, "Same," before showing him just how much I've missed him. Knowing we can't get carried away, I break our kiss and ask, "Did you help with everything you needed to this morning?"

"Yep. We have a few hours before we have to leave again.

How long will you need to get ready?" he asks, looping my arms around his neck.

I pretend to contemplate. "Hmmm... that depends..."

Running his fingers under my shirt he asks, "On?"

"On whether or not you're in the shower with me."

Lifting the hem of my shirt, he grins. "I'll make you a deal. We set the alarm for an hour, and then we'll be responsible adults and shower *separately* when it goes off. I'll even be a gentleman and let you go first."

"That's only because you know we'll never make it to the wedding otherwise," I tease, reaching for the hem of my shirt to drag it over my head. Ryan reaches behind me and unclasps my bra, letting it drop to the floor.

"Alexa," Ryan's voice carries throughout the room, "set an alarm for one hour."

While I work at the button of my shorts, he steps back from me and rips his shirt over his head. Then hastily shucks his gym shorts and boxers all before the animated voice can respond, "Alarm set for one hour."

When both of us are naked, I watch Ryan grip his hard cock and stroke it as he demands, "Get on the bed."

I don't have to be told twice.

Scurrying up the bed, I turn to see Ryan stalking toward me. The moment his knee makes the bed dip, my inner muscles clench and desire flows through me.

As he crawls up the bed to settle between my body, my legs part inviting him in.

"Are you wet for me, Lanie? "he asks as his finger trails along my inner thigh.

"Why don't you see for yourself," I challenge, hoping like hell he'll give me some relief soon.

Hovering over me, he props himself up on one arm, while the other continues to taunt and tease me, making me beg, "Ryan, I need you inside me."

"Patience," he whispers as his finger traces a circle around the entrance of my slit. "I wanna feel you first. Close your eyes and tell me what you feel."

The moment my eyes close, his lips brush a feathery kiss against mine.

When I don't answer, his finger stops. "Lanie?"

"Don't stop," I beg.

'Then tell me?" he coaxes by continuing his circular motion.

"Your breath is warm on my face. Your kiss felt soft, yet firm on my lips. You taste..." When his finger slowly dips in, then slides out, I cry out, "Oh, yes, Ryan. Right there."

Without missing a beat he feathers kisses across my body as he adds another finger. Instead of keeping them in the same rhythm, each time he dips in, he spreads them apart, in a scissor motion, making my body come alive. In and out, back and forth, he finds a rhythm that has the energy in my spine starting to pool.

When he kisses across my chest and down my abdomen, I feel like I might combust in anticipation. My muscles clench and my body stiffens the moment his tongue swipes along my slit and around my clit.

Flattening his tongue he flicks at my clit as his fingers work my pussy into a frenzy. The second he reaches up and plays my nipple between his finger and thumb, I fly over the edge of no return. Pulse after pulse of electric currents flow from my spine, reaching from my head to my toes.

"Ohmigod, Ryan. Right there," I pant as he continues like a man on a mission to milk every last twitch out of me.

"You taste fucking amazing," he says, crawling up my body. When we're face-to-face, he's got a goofy grin that's infectious. "How do you feel?"

"Like my body has a consistency of Jell-O." I laugh. "But it's the best possible feeling—ever." Reaching for his face, I pull him close and kiss him. He tastes of me. He tastes of him. It's something I need more of.

Before I know it our bodies are entwined with one another and his rock-hard cock is pressing into me. Reaching between us, I stroke him from root to tip and swirl his precum around the tip.

"You keep doing that, I'm not gonna last," he warns.

"Please tell me you have condoms," I tease, hoping like hell he does.

Reaching for the bedside drawer, he brings out an entire sleeve. "I've got plenty."

Sitting up, I take a condom from him and rip open the package. "Good. Let's get this on you."

Apparently, I'm too slow because he grabs the condom from my hand and has himself ready before I can even move. Stroking himself a few times, he asks with a playful smirk, "Top or bottom?"

"Hmmm... decisions... decisions," I tease and he takes matters into his own hands by rolling me onto my back.

It doesn't take him long to line up our bodies. Just as he enters me, he says, "Next time, you can be on top."

He takes his time at first, making sure I adjust to his size. The moment he's fully inside, he groans, "You feel so fucking good. I wanna stay like this forever, but I need to move."

Rocking my hips up, he meets me thrust for thrust. Loving the feel of his body on mine, I scrape my fingers down his back and grip his firm ass. "Harder," I beg.

When he lifts one of my legs onto his shoulder, it changes our position and he goes even deeper than before. "Oh, yes... right there," I beg as I chase my second orgasm of the day.

Ryan quickly finds a rhythm that has my entire body on fire. White heat courses through me and every muscle stiffens. After a few pumps, my entire body shatters. The moment my orgasm starts, he pumps twice into me and his entire body turns to granite as he pulses into the condom.

I love the feel of him as his body collapses onto mine, and we enjoy the aftershocks. Eventually, he rolls off me and goes to take care of the condom. But when he returns, he grins like the Cheshire cat and says, "Come on. I'm dying to take another shower with you."

Thinking of our last time I grin. "Well... we do have time."

*****

The minute we arrive at the ceremony, Ryan's greeted by his best friend Vince. They one-arm hug one another and slap each other on the back, the way men do. When he pulls back, he quickly makes introductions. "Vince, I'd like you to meet

Lanie." Taking my hand, he smiles wide. "Lanie, this is Vince, brother of the bride."

"It's nice to meet you, Lanie. Do you attend CRU? I swear I've seen you before."

"Yeah." I nod. "You look familiar, but I can't for the life of me place it."

"I swear, this world keeps getting smaller," Ryan grumbles. "But I had to go all the way back home to finally meet her."

"Well, at least your paths crossed," a beautiful redhead interjects as she clasps hands with Vince. "Hi, I'm Sydney. It's nice to finally meet you, Lanie."

Both Ryan and Vince give her a, *'would you shut up'* look and it's obvious there's been more than just my name said among them.

Brushing them off, she says, "Oh, hush. She knows what I mean. I've been dying to meet the girl that has Ryan's attention."

"Unks, we need you," comes from an adorable girl all decked out as a flower girl in a white poofy dress.

Turning, he kisses Sydney on the cheek. "That's our cue. Sorry, gotta run. I gotta give my sister away."

"Good luck, man; give Vanessa a hug for me."

"Will do." Vince nods and disappears into the house.

As I look around at the guests now taking their seats, I finally spot the groom. He stands under the trellis with an older man holding a bible and two men that have to be his brothers. They're just too similar to not be related.

Ryan squeezes my hand as the music begins. The bridesmaids and flower girl make their way down the aisle.

Then everyone stands as Vince appears with the stunning bride.

Every bride should only dream of looking this good on their wedding day. Her smile is infectious as she sees her groom waiting for her. You can feel their love from across the yard as she glides to him.

To my surprise, before Vince can give her away, the officiant who looks like he could be my grandpa has a few pointed words to say to the groom. "Now, Damien, Vanessa is a precious girl."

Damien nods in agreement, but the officiant continues. "Now her brother Vince may be giving her away, but if you pull any funny business, *I'll* be the one takin' care of things. Remember, I grew up in the South and I *know* how to hide a body."

Oh my god, did he really just say that? The entire yard waits on bated breath for Damien's response.

But the little flower girl pipes up for all of us to hear, "Really? Will you teach me that trick? I *always* get caught in hide and seek."

Holy shit. That is priceless. I'm not sure where to look first. Everyone's shocked expression feeds off one another. Once the groom laughs, the entire yard roars with laughter. Some are doubled over; others wipe tears from their cheeks.

That girl is a riot. When everyone calms down, she punches her fist to her waist irritated that everyone was laughing I'm sure. "Well, Jack, will ya teach me how to hide 'em?"

Bless that man's heart, he schools his features and nods. "When you're older, darling, I'll show you just where to go."

After the crowd settles again, the rest of the wedding goes by in a blur. That officiant kept this bridal party on their toes as he zipped off one-liners when you least expected it. By the time the bride and groom kissed, and everyone walked back down the aisle, my side hurt form laughing so much.

Ryan and I helped move chairs from the ceremony to the tables on the other side of the yard for the reception. Correct that, I moved my chair, and the groomsmen and a few of the guys I recognize from the basketball team had them all moved before the rest of us could think about it.

Before I know it, the reception's in full swing. There's dancing, lots of food and drinks. Ryan's talking with a group of guys near the bar and I'm sitting at a table with Sydney, Margo, the bride's best friend, and a girl by name of Chloe. Vanessa's dancing with her father-in-law and Jules and we're just enjoying the show.

Sydney looks to me and grins. "I'm so glad you're here with Ryan. It's great to see him *finally* dating."

Margo pipes in, "I'm glad you're here to help him through it all."

Repeating their words in my head, I finally have to ask, "What do you mean?"

Margo laughs once, then says, "For the longest time he's had a crush on Vanessa." Then she adds conspiratorially, "*Of course, she was none the wiser.*"

I look to Ryan who's talking with Vince, Damien, and the other groomsmen.

"Ryan's always been the sweetest guy," Sydney chimes in.

Chloe looks to the group of guys, one in particular she's been staring at all night long and sighs, "I'm not sure I'd be brave enough to go to the wedding of my longest crush."

"No kidding." Margo laughs, then glances at the group of guys. There's one in particular that's had her attention tonight, but I can't remember if his name is Tre or DeShawn. All I know is he's a basketball player, going to Boston Law next fall.

When Vanessa joins the group of guys, I watch as Ryan pulls her in for a hug. He says something to her and she laughs. Then she says something in return to him. When she turns her attention to Damien, I watch as Ryan shakes his head and looks away.

Holy shit. It's Vanessa.

She's the girl who's held his heart since freshman year.

Words he said to convince me to come tonight flood my mind.

There's nothing I won't do for either of them.

Holy shit, he brought me here to be his buffer.

When Ryan steps inside, I say to the table, "Will you excuse me, I need to use the restroom."

They pay me no attention, as they've moved on to Margo's date for the night.

Thankfully, I don't run into Ryan as I slip into the house and grab my purse from the room I'd left it in.

Needing air, and to think, I slip out the front door.

Pulling up the app on my phone, I think of calling a car, but I don't want to stick around in case Ryan decides to look for me. Instead, I make the hasty decision to walk the two miles back to my car.

Walking doesn't help.

My mind comes up with a million reasons why Ryan brought me as his date.

It's obvious that he still cares about her. What was his point in bringing me?

Did he make me fall for him, just to make it believable?

By the time I get to my car, all I want to do is go to the one place where I feel safe. The place I feel loved. The place I call home.

Chapter 23
Ryan

DAMIEN HAD WANTED help bringing out more beer to the cooler. But when I return, Lanie's nowhere to be found. I look through the house once more before going to the table of girls I'd left her with earlier.

"Do you know where Lanie is?" I ask, scanning the crowd.

"Last I saw, she got up to use the bathroom a few minutes ago."

Sydney stands. "Want me to help look for her?"

"No. I was just inside, maybe we crossed paths without knowing."

Walking to the main bathroom, I'm frustrated to find it empty. When Vince walks in, I ask, "Hey, is there another bathroom? The girls said Lanie went inside to use it, but she's just not anywhere I can find her."

"Look, I'm sure she's around. I'll go check the master

bathroom, you make one more sweep through the house and yard. We'll meet back outside in a few minutes."

When Vince returns empty-handed, I do what I should've done to begin with.

I pull out my phone and text.

Me: Where are you?

I see the message go from sent, to delivered, to read.

I watch eagerly as the three little dots bounce around, then my heart sinks when they disappear.

Me: Look. I'm worried. Can you at least tell me if you're okay?

Again, the message is sent, delivered, and read.

When only two words are returned, my stomach drops to the floor.

Lanie: I'm fine.

Two words, no man ever wants to hear—especially from a woman.

Not wanting to ruin the party for my friends, I pay my respect to the bride and groom, then tell Vince I'm heading out.

He can tell something's off, but I assure him I've got it handled.

Knowing there are a million places on campus she could be, I go home, hoping like hell, she'll meet me there.

As I drive into my complex, my chest squeezes tighter when I see there's another car parked in the spot that held Lanie's car when she left.

Climbing the stairs, I'm at a loss for what to do.

Do I stay here in case she returns? Do I go out to look for her? Or do I drive back to Seaside?

If I try sending another text, will she respond?

Me: Where are you?

Again, Sent. Delivered. Read.

Me: Seriously, Melanie. Where are you? I'm going out of my mind worrying about you. Should I call your parents? The police? Please. I won't bother you. But I need to know you're safe.

My heart nearly beats out of my chest as I await a response—any response would be better than the agony of not knowing.

Lanie: I'm fine. I'm safe. No need to call anyone. Just getting air.

Just getting air?

Just getting air.

I can't fucking breathe and she's just getting air!

What the fuck does that even mean?

When midnight rolls around and I still haven't heard from her, I leave my apartment door unlocked, hoping by some miracle she comes back.

When I can't pace any longer, I trudge into my room, undress by my bed, slip into the sheets, and turn off the light.

Fuck, even the bedsheets smell like her.

I toss and turn for what feels like hours before I finally fall into a restless sleep.

When I wake up the next morning, I feel like I have a hangover—without any of the fun. I only had one beer last night, but I wish I'd drowned my sorrows, so I just wouldn't feel. Because what I feel right now—is like complete shit.

When she hasn't returned by ten o'clock the next morning, I return to Seaside. I should've gone back last night I'm almost certain that's where she is now. But at the time I'd been holding out hope that she'd return.

As I drive a hundred miles back to the beach, one thought runs through my mind.

I've given you your space, Melanie Lancaster—ready or not here I come.

Chapter 24
Ryan

THE MOMENT I get into town, I drive straight to Lanie's. It's a little after noon when I arrive. Stomping up the steps, I pound on the front door.

When no one answers, I rap three more times.

"I'm coming... I'm coming..." can be heard from the other side in a groggy voice.

Unfortunately, it's Lizzy who answers the door. "What's goin' on, Ryan?" she mutters groggily. Obviously, I've woken her up. But at this point, my give-a-fuck is broken and I need to see Lanie.

"Is Lanie here?" I demand.

"I... I'm not sure," Lizzy says, scratching her head on a yawn.

From behind her, I hear Raven. "She's not in her room, but she came home late last night."

"Do you know where she is?" I pin her eyes, hoping she'll grant me mercy.

"I'm pretty sure she went for a walk," Sloane says, joining her sisters at the door.

Sloane and Raven cross their arms over their chests and I can tell if I act like a complete asshat, we're going to be at a stalemate.

"Look, I have no idea what the fuck is even going on. One minute we were at my friend's wedding, the next minute she disappears and ghosts me. I asked her if she was okay—she said she was 'fine' when clearly, she's not. Then when I threatened to call her family or go to the police, she told me she was okay and going for some air."

When each of them remains in stony silence, I go for broke.

"She claims she was going for *air*. Air—can you fucking believe that? I haven't been able to fucking breathe since she left. She took my fucking heart with her and I need to find her and make this right."

"What did you do to make her need it?"

Throwing my hands in the air, I shout, "That's just it! One minute we were enjoying the evening, the next she was just fucking gone—saying she needed air. I've been going out of my mind since she left."

"What do you want us to do?" Sloane asks skeptically.

"Hell, I don't know. I just need to know if she's okay."

For the longest moment, no one moves—and we just stare at one another.

Lanie steps around the corner from the hall and says, "It's okay, girls. I'll talk to him."

Relief floods through me. For the first time since the wedding, I finally can breathe.

Her eyes are puffy and her face blotchy. She's obviously been crying, but at least she's willing to talk.

Her sisters are hesitant, but one by one, they walk away without a word.

My voice is hoarse when I rasp out, "Why?"

"I need to ask you the same thing," she states solemnly.

As if I wasn't already confused, I ask, "What are you talking about?"

"Why did you invite me to the wedding?"

Cocking my head to the side, hoping for a better view into that brain of hers, I'm frustrated I still need to clarify. "What. Do. You. Mean?"

"Why did you bring me as your date to *that wedding*, specifically?"

"Because you are my girlfriend."

When it's obvious this isn't going to cut it for her, I continue, "Because I didn't want to spend another weekend away from you."

Nope, still not enough for her. Her expression is bleak and completely unreadable. But she asks again, "Why did you invite me to *Vanessa's* wedding?"

Where is she going with this? The way she says Vanessa's name makes me pause before continuing.

"What about Vanessa?"

"Is she the one you've been in love with since freshman

year? The one that you watched fall in love with someone else? The one you'd do anything for?"

Oh, fuck. Now it all makes sense.

Sighing, I try to figure out where to begin. After what feels like an eternity of silence, I find my words. "Yes, but you've got it all wrong.

"When I met Vince and Vanessa freshman year, they had just lost their parents, and basically their entire life as they knew it. He was determined to get her through school because Jules, Vanessa's daughter, needed the best life she could get.

"When I met Vanessa, I'll admit I was attracted to her. We got along as friends and that's all we ever were because she had too much to deal with to even think about dating so I was gladly friend zoned.

"Someday, well... you'll have to hear their story from them because it's not my place to tell. But the long and the short of it is that it was easy for me to fixate on the unavailable because then I never had to put my heart out there. I could be the friend, pine for the girl. But I was never the one for her.

"It took a while, but once I finally saw her look at him like he was the sun, moon, and stars all wrapped up in one, it was all it took for me to realize I wasn't the one for her.

"It was a hard pill to swallow, but in that one instance, I knew without a doubt I wasn't in love with her. What I felt for her was infatuation and desire for the unobtainable. I won't lie to you. I do love her, but as a friend like I should have all along.

"If you take the time to learn her backstory, I'm sure you will, too. She and Vince have been dealt a shitty hand in life, but they're making the best of it. I said I will do *anything* for the two of them because I am *literally* one of the few people who've become their built-in family. For years they only had each other and Jules, and I will do what I can to make their lives better. Period."

"So you're not in love with her?" comes out as a whisper.

Needing her to hear this, I firmly state, "No. I'm not."

"How do you know you're not in love with her?"

Thank fuck. Finally, an easy question.

Grinning I take a step toward Lanie. "Because I've fallen head over heels in love with you, Melanie Lancaster."

Taking another step forward, "I want to spend time with you, and because even in this short amount of time we've been together, I feel like I need you almost as much as I need my next breath."

Finally, we're standing toe-to-toe and it takes everything in me to keep what little distance there is between us.

"That's good," she sighs.

When she places her hand on my cheek and smiles, I have to ask, "Why is that good?"

"Because I love you, Ryan."

Grinning wide, I swoop her into my arms and murmur, "Those quite possibly might be the five best words I've ever heard," before crashing my lips onto hers.

EPILOGUE

Sloane

One year later...

Watching my sister fall in love last summer gave me something I hadn't expected—hope. It gave me hope that there might be someone out there for me and hope that I might get past my misguided fears and finally let someone in.

With my help, Ryan's planning the most epic proposal. I just have to get the know-it-all musician I work with to fall in line to make it work.

Jax is wicked smart, extremely talented, and sexy as sin. But he can't see the forest for the trees when it comes to his potential. He'd rather keep playing in dive bars along the coast than take a real shot at success.

When the Seaside festival has a music competition, I present Jax with an ultimatum that will either make or break both our careers.

I've laid it all on the line, but can he?

The End

THIS MAY BE the end of Lanie and Ryan's story in The Summer Dare, but it is not the end of the Lancaster sisters' stories. Find out what happens to Sloane and Jax next in The Summer Ultimatum – is Now Available. Start reading their story today: https://books2read.com/SummerDare

AUTHOR'S NOTE: If you like reading books set in one world, you'll be happy to find several full-length stories for several of the characters mentioned in this story already written and available on my website www.amandashelley.com

BE sure you stay up to date with all things Amanda Shelley by joining my newsletter: https://geni.us/AmandaShelleyNL

ABOUT THE AUTHOR

Amanda Shelley writes romantic stories you can escape into. Some are steamy, others are sweet but all have strong characters with a little bit of sass.

When not writing, Amanda enjoys time with her family, playing chauffeur, chef and being an enthusiastic fan for her children. Keeping up with them keeps her alert and grounded in reality. She enjoys long car rides, chai lattes and popping her SUV into four-wheel drive for adventures anywhere.

Amanda loves hearing from readers. Be sure to sign up for her newsletter and follow her on social media. Join her reader's group Amanda's Army of Readers to stay up to date on her latest information.

Readers group: https://www.facebook.com/groups/Amandas
ArmyofReaders/
Goodreads: https://www.goodreads.com/author/show/
19713563.Amanda_Shelley
Newsletter: https://geni.us/AmandaShelleyNL
www.amandashelley.com

ACKNOWLEDGMENTS

First, I would like to thank you the reader, blogger, and reviewer for taking the time to read this book. There are so many stories to choose from, and I'm humbly honored you've chosen to read mine. I hope you enjoyed Ryan and Lanie's story. If you want more from the from their word, be sure to check out the Perfectly Independent Series.

I'd love to hear from you and your thoughts about Derek and Tessa. You can find me on social media, my reader's group *Amanda's Army of Readers*, or at www.amandashelley.com. If you care to share your thoughts on this book with other book lovers, please consider leaving a review at any of the retail sites or on Goodreads, BingeBooks, and BookBub.

I'd like to thank C.L. Collier for being my partner in crime and making the Summer in Seaside Series come to life. She helped make this random thought I had one day, turn into an amazing multi-author collaboration. She

I'd also like to thank the authors in this series for taking a chance on us as collaborators and taking this journey with us. I couldn't be prouder of what we accomplished together!

This book wouldn't be what it is without my amazing team of support. To Renita McKinney at A Book A Day Author Services, thank you for helping me develop Ryan and Lanie's characters and make them into the best they can be. Thanks so much for having my back and making this happen.

To Julie Deaton at Deaton Author Services, thanks for making my book pretty and talking me off a ledge. I appreciate knowing your proofreading is exquisite, and my worries disappear. Your eagle eyes are spectacular, and I don't know what I'd do without you.

To the people who have supported me along the way, I'm humbly grateful to have you in my life. Whether you've read my books, asked me about my progress, listened to me talk about my fictional characters as if they're a part of my family, plotted with me, or been my cheerleader, I appreciate your continued support. Please know it hasn't gone unnoticed.

Last but certainly not least, to my four beautiful girls who have had to wait patiently when I said, "Just one more minute," when I obviously meant a lot more than one. I love that you get that I have deadlines and will sometimes keep me on task with your not-so-subtle reminders that "Mom... you should be working" during my designated times. I appreciate your support more than you'll ever know. Even though you can't read this book—because that might be *weird*—for both of us, I love that you keep asking. I love you all more than words can express. You're the reason I continue to strive and reach for my goals each day.

If you enjoyed this book, you will be happy to discover Amanda Shelley primarily writes in one world. For a complete list of the series reading order as well as a chronological time line, please visit:

https://amandashelley.com/reading-order/

The Summer Ultimatum

Watching my sister fall in love last summer gave me something I hadn't expected—hope. It gave me hope that there might be someone out there for me and hope that I might get past my misguided fears and finally let someone in.

With my help, Ryan's planning the most epic proposal. I just have to get the know-it-all musician I work with to fall in line to make it work.

Jax is wicked smart, extremely talented, and sexy as sin. But he can't see the forest for the trees when it comes to his potential. He'd rather keep playing in dive bars along the coast than take a real shot at success.

When the Seaside festival has a music competition, I present Jax with an ultimatum that will either make or break both our careers.

I've laid it all on the line, but can he?

https://geni.us/AmandaShelleyBooks

The Summer Proposal

My sisters are dropping like flies.

They're falling in love and having the time of their lives.

Don't get me wrong, I'm ecstatic for them. I love seeing them happy.

But I'm not ready for that type of commitment.

I can't even keep a plant alive, let alone find someone worthy of getting past a third date.

As the only sister done with school and single as a pringle, I have to do something fast, or I'll be my matchmaking aunt's next victim.

When Jax's drummer joins him for the summer and needs some help with his image, I make him a deal he can't refuse.

All is perfect—until I realize my summer proposal has one minor flaw.

Our relationship may be a sham, but there's nothing fake about my feelings for Finn.

https://geni.us/AmandaShelleyBooks

The Summer Arrangement

One, two, three—it's all down to me.

As the youngest and only single Lancaster, I'm eager to spend my summer in Seaside, Oregon, with my sisters. It's something I've looked forward to all year, and I'm determined to make every minute count. After all, I've only got one year before I graduate from college and have to adult for real.

However, if I want to graduate debt free, I need to work. I have a lead on the perfect summer job with the nanny agency I've spent the last three summers catering to.

I just have to win over an adorable three-year-old and convince her single dad I'm the right one for the job.

Simple enough, right?

Except when I show up at his door, I'm shocked to find he's the guy I hooked up with a few times last semester.

This cannot be happening.

I need this job. There's too much on the line to walk away. Maybe we can put the past behind us and make some sort of summer arrangement?

https://geni.us/AmandaShelleyBooks

The Summer I Found Home

Being a pilot is all I've ever known.

I served my country and I'm damn proud of my career.

But sacrifices were made, especially when it came to family.

I've missed first steps, first days of school, and first dates to name a few.

My kids grew up. They're having families of their own.

Was it worth it?

When an opportunity brings me to Seaside, I jump feet first no questions asked.

It means experiencing all those firsts with my grandkids.

With family as my focus and my guard down, I don't even see Faye coming.

She's a force to be reckoned with and has me holding on for dear life.

I thought our ship had sailed, but now that I'm home for good—I just might get more than one second chance.

arrangement?

https://geni.us/AmandaShelleyBooks

Zander: A Perfectly Independent Series Novella

(Available for free on All Retailers)

Zander's known for being a player both on and off the court. When his name shows up as my next client, my heart stalls, and not in a good way. There's no way I'll survive the semester with him. I just don't have the patience.

However, when I need help, Zander makes a proposal I can't refuse. He'll be my fake date to my best friend's wedding so I don't have to face my ex and his new girlfriend alone.

The weekend goes off without a hitch as we effortlessly pretend to have the time of our lives.

All is perfect... until I realize my feelings for Zander are no longer an act.

What will I do when our arrangement comes to an end?

https://geni.us/AmandaShelleyBooks

Drew: Book One of the Perfectly Independent Series

Of all people, why him?

He didn't EVEN bother introducing himself, just assumed I knew him from his fame on the court.

I nearly died on the spot when our professor announced we were permanent lab partners. Between his arrogance and the constant interruption from basketball groupies, there's no way I'll survive this semester.

Sure, he's hotter than anyone I've ever seen in a science lab with his sexy blue eyes, cute dimple, and muscles for days - but I can't afford *his* kind of distractions.

Okay. Deep breath.

I can do this.

After all, it's only one semester.

Just when I think my self-control is in check, he does something to show me that he isn't the egotistical, self-centered jerk I thought he was.

How can his stupid smile suddenly make my mind melt, heart race, and palms sweat?

If I take this chance on Drew, will my perfectly laid out plans disappear?

https://geni.us/AmandaShelleyBooks

Vince: Book Two of the Perfectly Independent Series

It's funny how one night can change everything.

As a bartender near campus, I'm certain I've heard it all. Rarely a shift passes without some guy taking his best shot, hoping I'll end my self-proclaimed dating diet.

Of course, this is exactly how I meet Vince.

Except, he isn't the one running his mouth.

No, he simply shuts down his idiotic friend, then stops my heart with the simplest of smiles and walks away.

Just when I force myself to forget him, he bumps into me on campus.

Our connection is consuming, and my world is knocked off kilter. It's far beyond physical attraction. He's smart, sexy, and feels like—home?

Wait, that can't be right...

Whatever it is, Vince has me breaking my rules to spend time with him.

My entire life I've prepared for meeting the wrong guys.

What the hell should I do when I find the right one?

https://geni.us/AmandaShelleyBooks

Damien: Book Three of the Perfectly Independent Series

Beautiful girls are not hard to find at Columbia River University.

The coeds on campus are great to look at but I was over that scene after graduation three years ago.

These days, outside of being part of the largest civil engineering job on campus, all I'm searching for is a decent meal and some peace and quiet. It's why I'm happy to have found what I consider a hidden gem in the diner I frequent.

All I need to do is finish this job and move on to the next by year's end.

Should be easy enough. Only when Vanessa walks up with a sexy smile and a mouth full of sass, she does more than take my order. She completely takes my breath away.

Next thing I know, I'm here every morning, making every excuse to dine with this intriguing woman. Not only is she smart and sexy, but she's laser focused on reaching the goals she's set for herself.

The more I get to know her, the more I'm convinced she's the one. I just have to find a way to get her to deviate from her perfectly laid plans and take a chance on me.

https://geni.us/AmandaShelleyBooks

Making The Call

Dani

As a bestselling romance author, most assume my life's glamorous, filled with combustible chemistry, and most of all, romance. Ha! I can only wish. With a deadline looming, I've escaped to my family's cabin on Anderson Island to free myself from distractions. My plan's great, until a man, who could pass as a cover model on one of my books, comes to my rescue. Is there chemistry? Sure. Is he everything I'd look for in a guy? Absolutely. But will my career be at risk if I give into my desire?

Luke

For a player, women line up outside the locker room. For coaches, we're lucky to get in the game. As the youngest NFL coach in the league, I live, eat, breathe, and even sleep football. To gear up for this season, I return to my home on Anderson Island for a much-needed break. When Dani literally crashes into my life, my mind's suddenly on the sexy brunette with a sailors mouth, rather than my team's next play. She has me dusting off another playbook entirely, making me wonder, did I make the right call?

https://geni.us/AmandaShelleyBooks

The Boy Upstairs

I ran into Derek while trying to escape the neighbor from hell.

Instantly, we hit it off. Since he's only here for three months and the microbrewery leaves me little time for commitments, it's the perfect setup for a fling.

He's adventurous, challenges me, and he just gets me from the inside out.

With our expiration date quickly approaching, I'm left to wonder... Will my heart ever be the same without the boy upstairs?

https://geni.us/AmandaShelleyBooks

He Saved My Boy

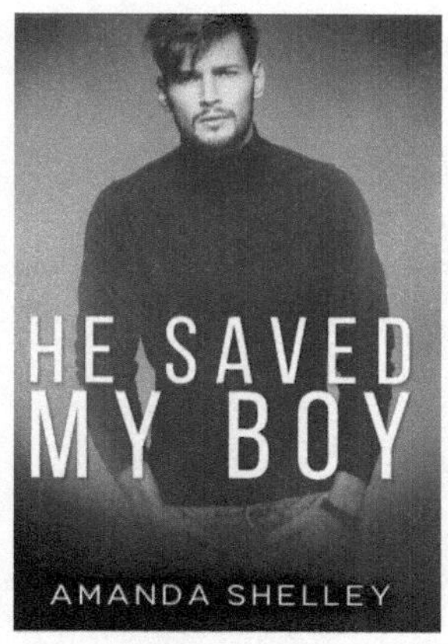

Davis is the first guy to catch my attention since... hell, I don't even know.

Instantly, he makes me think and feel things I've forgotten existed. It has been forever since I put my needs first, so I take the chance and let him light me up from the inside out.

Our night is the kind that will ruin me for all others.

But then I get the dreaded call.

I rush out without a second glance, knowing I'll likely never see him again.

My son will always come first—Always.

Imagine my surprise when Davis walks in, and I find he's the only one who can save my boy.

This cannot be happening—*I guess it's time to pull up my big girl panties and see what happens.*

https://geni.us/AmandaShelleyBooks

The Vegas Pitch

This pitch could make or break my career.

Not only will it set a personal record for the biggest account I've ever landed, but it could set my newfound company three years ahead of schedule for expansion.

Thank god I've got Nate Bellinger on my team.

Even though I had my reservations hiring the sexiest man I've ever laid eyes on – he more than meets my expectations with his hard work and determination. Together, we've formed a solid team and play off each other perfectly.

As we wait for the final verdict, I begrudgingly take Nate up on his offer for a night on the town. After all, this is Vegas and I need to let the chips fall where they may.

Imagine my surprise when I wake up the next morning to find we've not only won the campaign, but I'm apparently married to the man I've only ever let myself fantasize about.

The kicker of it all – he has no intentions of letting me go.

But what will it mean once we leave Vegas?

Resilience: Book One of Resilience Duet

Resolution: Book Two of Resilience Duet

Samantha never saw Enzo coming.

As the dust settles from her divorce, her life is full. She doesn't have time for distractions. She's too busy running her own company and checking off numerous items from her kids' demanding schedule to have a life of her own.

Then he walks into her kitchen with his breathtaking green eyes and a mischievous grin. He's there to surprise his father - her contractor, but his presence makes everything off kilter.

Enzo's perfectly content with his adventurous life as an elite rescue pilot, until a harmless prank turns on him. Instead of surprising his father, he finds his world thrown off course by the beautiful woman with a sexy smile, wicked sass and the mouthwatering ability to keep him on his toes.

With his limited time on leave, is she worth the risk to his heart?

https://geni.us/AmandaShelleyBooks

Collide: A Sweet Romance

Falling head over heels was the last thing I expected.

Literally.

Coffee is everywhere – and more than my ego is bruised.

When the handsome stranger I plowed into calls me by name, mortification sinks in.

He rushes off to class. I run home to change, hoping to forget the whole incident.

If only I could be so lucky.

I quickly find it's a small world and Gavin Wallace is completely unavoidable. Everywhere I turn he's there. In my classes. Hanging with my friends.

I've got his full attention and I have to admit, I like it a lot more than I should.

https://geni.us/AmandaShelleyBooks